CULT MAGNETISM

I0533793

JASON TEJIRI BOJE

CULT MAGNETISM

Copyright © 2024 by Jason Boje

Second Edition: November 2025

Self-Published by: Jason Boje

Cover Design by: Jason Boje

Interior Layout by: Jason Boje

DEGENERATE, GRADUATE

THE 2020s. A period that historians of Alterna-Earth looked back on with intrigue and sorrow. The first half was infamous for being the beginning of the CM Era. This was the decade in which the people of their world saw their lives permanently changed by magnetism, in both senses of the word. The impact of the first meaning was more than obvious to most. The pervasiveness of the second would take a while before it was noticed on a grand scale.

The Lord giveth and the Lord taketh away. A biblical expression many humans of many civilisations were greatly familiar with, both in speech and practice. Though at times, the expression was flipped. The millions of lives taken away by the unholy matrimony of worldwide quakes and the sporadic sprawling of volcanic doom were forgotten once what was left in their wake was discovered. A never-before-seen natural phenomenon in which a potently useful substance was spread across lands to be found and mined. Slaekrock, a vantablack metallic naturally occurring rock from fine soil just below the surface, saw itself altered by molten lava in a process that could be described as nothing short of magical.

Never before had a material been found to be so hard yet so malleable. So rigid and yet possessing such magnetic properties. So wonderful yet so dangerous.

Meddling with Slaekrock led to the invention of a new product that held the world in a vice. The aptly named *Slaek Devices*. A vantablack ring one could slide onto their wrist or place on their walls or floors, using its immense attraction properties for their daily lives, activated by a flick of the wrist, a curl of the fingers, or, if high-level enough, immediately upon placement. If one could get their hands on such a product, they could utilise telekinetic abilities in the comfort of their homes. What use was there in going downstairs to fix yourself a meal when you could float a plate up to your room with ease? By the year 2022 AE, the type of technology previously reserved for military personnel and government officials, the type of technology that one would only ever hear news stories about over the years, could just as easily be placed in the hands of an average Joe. Slaek Devices revolutionised every aspect of the world, from mundane public transportation to great voyages beyond the stars. For a moment, it seemed as if the humanity of Alterna-Earth had acted upon what was to be the next step of their evolution. For a moment, the constant progress and prosperity promised to the people of the world seemed to be set in stone, courtesy of the devices that allowed for acts of great magic.

Only for a moment. Then, reality hit.

***

Few despised Slaek Devices and how common they were becoming in 2022 AE. A select number of youth. This was highly ironic considering some of these people were part of the demographic they advertised to most frequently.

Desmond Eze was a handsome, dark-skinned, well-to-do, university-educated young man with a sharp jaw and sharper eyes. He saw people who looked like him on billboards and in-between ad breaks when he watched videos online, insisting he buy as many Slaek Devices as possible. It only made Desmond more disgusted by the thought of buying those damned black bracelets. Especially when he thought of how such technology was being used in the Ivrear area.

One evening, Desmond walked down a pothole-ridden road outside his childhood neighbourhood in his hometown. He grunted as he kicked over rubble from one of these craters.

"They can give us telekinesis, but they can't give us working roads?" Desmond scoffed.

As he trudged down the empty road, he caught wind of an all-too-common sight in his cherished hometown. A group of thugs were crowded together in a side street. Most of these men wore some form of white vest and football shorts combination. All faces between these moist, mould-plastered walls that sectioned the side street wore countenances of vehemence or indignation. Of the eight men who had gathered for the conflict occurring, Desmond counted guns in five of their hands. But an even more dangerous device was fixed on the wrists of some of these thugs. Bootleg Slaek Devices. Jagged, rudimentary versions of the real deal, colloquially known as *Roef Devices*.

Desmond paused his walk to watch the scene unfold from afar. He knew he was about to witness reason number one hundred as to why he disliked Slaek Devices.

An uncoordinated spectacle of bullets and blood flying through the dirty streets commenced. One of the thugs had attempted to use his device to float the gun out of his rival's hand. The second rival used his Roef to telekinetically pull

3

the gun back, only to accidentally yank the trigger and blast his face to fleshy smithereens. The first rival laughed but was quickly dealt with for such mockery with a few bullets to the chest, courtesy of the second rival's companion letting loose with his rifle. What followed was a messy gun fight that hardly anyone could keep track of. The two dead thug leaders had their bootleg Slaek Devices ripped from their hands in a desperate effort to get the upper hand in the gunfight.

The result: all eight thugs dead, the streets panging with the copper stench of blood mixed with smoky gunpowder, and two Roef Devices scattered on the floor for the next thug to come over and pick up. Desmond had little to no reaction to this gruesome scene. All he could muster was a dejected sigh to go along with his apathy. That marked the third instance he saw of this nature that week.

As he made his way further down the road, he could not help but notice the lacklustre infrastructure around him. Greyish-brown one-story council houses, corner shops with missing doors, cars with their wheels stolen and lumps of molten rock put in their place. "It's one thing to return to depressing stagnation, it's another thing to see everything worsen," Desmond thought. "The whole city's a pothole."

The only thing of beauty to be seen in the general vicinity proved to be a worse eyesore in spirit. He saw a billboard where, instead of having an ad painted on it, a virtual image was projected. An image of another man shilling the same product range he saw everywhere. Another handsome, put-together young man with soulless eyes, insisting that "Every home should have Slaek! Don't be left behind! Join the world as we float towards a better future!"

"They can give us telekinesis, but they can't even give us better roads," Desmond repeated in a furious grumble.

A memory came to mind. He recalled having visited a friend a year prior and seeing what access to such technology had done to his father. He had always been a crass, albeit hardworking man, as industrious as a construction worker could be. Then, when the companies that hired him were granted access to Slaek, he and his fellow workers had their work replaced by one man using a high-level Slaek Device to telekinetically do all the tasks they could in half the time. All that friend's dad did nowadays was use the same tech that put him out of a job to float beers, getting drunker by the minute as he developed bed sores from being glued to his living room chair each day. A sad state of affairs, Desmond thought.

***

Desmond returned to his university flat the day following his hometown visit. He lazily swung the door open, taking one step into the rough carpeted floors before throwing himself onto his bed.

Even in the comfort of his cosy university room, all he could muster was a sigh. He emptily stared at the ceiling, as if he had already died in essence. One look at Desmond Eze in this state, followed by a glance around his bedroom, painted a contrasting picture of the type of man he was.

A polished wooden shelf of even more polished golden awards acted as the centrepiece of his room, displayed on the back wall between a window and a mahogany cupboard. Occupying this display were countless trophies with his name on them, noting his achievements in academics, mostly, with a few being athletic accolades of some sort. Accompanying the trophies were framed photos of Desmond in his earlier years of university. Some with him fraternising with key members of the university's faculty, members of Hercole's community centres, and the friends he had made along the way. The display painted a picture of the highly competent, highly charismatic, and effortlessly successful student and community member. A contrast to the lonely, apathetic, often depressed man who lay sprawled across the bed.

Desmond knew that in a few weeks, he would have more awards and photos to go along with the ones he stared at from across the room. He and a few other top students would be awarded during the Hercole University graduation ceremonies. There was once a time when such a prospect filled him with great excitement and anticipatory glory. The thought of it now only made him groan.

Desmond opened his phone and searched for the document of notes he had made years ago. He brought it up. Tilted, "*The five key goals I should achieve by graduation*":

1. Achieve stellar grades and *2. Have a series of notable awards and accolades to my name.* These were both goals he had *easily* achieved over the years. Then came the three goals he had not achieved wholly:

3. Have the perfect job lined up. He had spoken to quite a few recruiters, but it seemed that all the jobs he had his eyes on would be taken over by those possessing high-level Slaek Devices. Either a job he wanted would be taken over by a man subscribed to the magnetic draw of the devices that gripped his society, or he would have to become said man to earn high-level employment. Neither situation was ideal.

4. Form lifelong bonds I'll never forget. Some might glance at the many framed photos on his display shelf and assume this goal had been achieved. It had not. Most of these bonds were shallow relations formed for personal gain on his part or the other party's. He could count on one hand the number of actual friends he had made at Hercole University.

And 5. The final goal: *Make my parents proud. Proud enough to accept me once again. Proud enough to forgive their last surviving son for all he's done.*

That one went without saying. It remained thoroughly unachieved. In fact, of all of them, it was the one he was furthest from completing.

Desmond sighed, turning off his phone.

***

Weeks passed by, and so had most of the graduation ceremony from Desmond's perspective. Despite the great fanfare made of the event, he could not remember most of it, having disassociated the second he sat on the crimson seats of the great hall. Amongst the banners, ribbons, and flashing lights, high-grade Slaek Devices were attached to the top railings around the hall's high ceiling. This allowed for some intriguing shots to be taken by hovering cameras in the sky, as well as for each award and certificate granted to a student to be floated over to them on stage in a beautiful spectacle. Though he did not care much for it all, he had to admit it was interesting to watch. Desmond continued to dissociate throughout the ceremony, allowing his mind to take him anywhere but the present moment. He was only brought back once a big announcement was made.

"And now, I'd like to ask the following students to join me…" the announcer softly echoed into the microphone as he called out the names of a series of students, including Desmond, to rise from their seats and walk upon the stage. "…it is time we celebrate the most acclaimed students of this year's graduating class."

Minutes later, Desmond was on stage amongst the other top students of his graduating class. He straightened his back, putting on the demeanour of poised pride he was known for as he and his fellow high-achieving classmates accepted an uproarious round of applause. Following the applause, the Dean of Hercole University took centre stage. He gave a long-winded speech commending the achievement of that particular graduating class as more gold badges and certificates were floated from backstage and into the hands of the top students.

During this speech, Desmond's mind wandered again. As did his eyes as he observed the other students alongside him. Most were not worth watching for too long. They were the typical Hercole students. Good-looking faces, bold expressions, dressed in presentable suits and gowns, and somewhat empty behind the eyes.

Only one of these students held his interest. Margot Forster, an infamous student with whom he had crossed paths many times but would hardly consider a friend. He would sooner have expected to see this particular young woman grinding the night away in the seediest clubs and bars of the city centre rather than studying at the library or winning accolades in sports. And yet here she was, Margot Forster, a part of the elite class of top Hercole students.

As intelligent as her presence here indicated she was, he still could not believe she was occupying the same stage as him. He noted her beautiful mess of hair, poorly cut short. Faint scars on her neck and cheeks accompanied freckles that dotted her tanned skin. The perpetual irreverence held in her brownish-green eyes and sharp-toothed smile. She was the strangest person on stage. The most visually intriguing.

Desmond's split-second observation was enough to grasp her attention. Soon, she held eyes with him. The pair stared at each other for longer than he would have liked.

Margot's mischievous smile locked onto his empty gaze. Desmond attempted to break contact with her multiple times as the Dean's speech droned on in the background.

***

"Desmond?" he heard Margot call out to him after the graduation ceremony's conclusion.

The area had emptied by this point, the chairs having been cleared out of the hall and Slaek Devices removed from the ceiling spectacle ring. The only reason Desmond had stayed back that long was to talk with the students and lecturers who were curious to know the post-graduate plans of one of their university's best. All of which were beginning to leave after getting an unsatisfactory answer from the great Desmond Eze: "I'm not sure yet."

As Desmond sought to leave the hall, Margot had tugged at his graduation robe. The two locked eyes again.

"Margot," he answered as he turned to face her. "Can I help you with something?"

"No, but I can help you," Margot said.
Desmond disliked the smile that was creeping across her face as she bit the corner of her bottom lip.

Desmond sighed. "From the look on your face, I don't think I want whatever help you're offering."

Margot laughed. "Weren't you like, the #3 student in the entire uni grades-wise, Desmond?"

"I was. Why?"

"I overheard some of your conversations just then. A top-three student shouldn't have such a vague, wishy-washy idea of what he's going to do with himself in the future."

"Yeah, I've been told."

"What course did you do again, Des?"

"Analytic Management."

"There are a lot of job options for Analytic Management majors. A *lot*."

"Not unless you're both proficient in Slaek Device usage and able to purchase and maintain the highest-level equipment for it. Neither of which I am or will be very soon."

"It's better than other courses. A huge chunk of graduates won't even get a job in the first place. Their future roles have already been taken by those who, as you say, can purchase and use Slaek at the highest level. At least you have the chance to become one of those people," Margot explained.

"Much easier said than done. Not that it's any of your business," Desmond said.

Margot huffed a little giggle under her breath as she leaned against the wall. "So, you don't want my help then?" she asked, crossing her arms.

"You've not even told me what you plan on helping me with yet," Desmond said. "Tell me, instead of wasting time dancing around the topic."

Margot nodded as she reached into her pocket for her phone. She pulled up a photo to show him. It was an image of a pale, slick man in a suit discussing with students.

"You've seen him before, haven't you?" Margot asked.

"He's a job recruiter, isn't he?" Desmond asked, to which she nodded. "I had a few discussions with him on campus back in second year. Works for RealSlaek RF."

RealSlaek Research Firm was the number one company in terms of all things Slaek Device oriented, from the cultivation of materials needed for them and the ironing out of the construction, to their on-site sales and online product marketing. With them being the leading company in Slaek development, procurement, and distribution, students like Desmond heard a great deal about them. Especially due to the company's meteoric rise coinciding with their enrolment in university during the AE 2020s.

"I've had many discussions with that exact recruiter, too. The latest one ending in me getting a job there," Margot elaborated. "Your name came up during one of these conversations, you know. He says you were one of the other students here he really wanted to get a hold of, but you never answered his emails. Very rude if you ask me."

"Why the hell were you discussing me during your recruitment meeting?"

"Why does anyone do anything nowadays?"

Desmond's glare pierced at this response.

"Listen, like I said before, those types of jobs go to people already proficient in using the Slaek Devices, and they often don't subsidise people for maintaining them, not even graduates. I won't be able to purchase a device at a high enough level to do the types of jobs they offer there. And that was *if* I even wanted to."

"Yeah, that's the whole point of what I'm helping you with, dummy. You won't need to do all of that nonsense with the deal I got for you," Margot retorted.

"What deal?"

Margot cleared her throat obnoxiously. "What I've gotten for you, dear Desmond, is a solid offer for a special job that won't require that much Slaek usage. Just someone with an analytical mind and a willingness to grind shit out," Margot said. "From what I've heard, that sounds like the perfect job for someone like you."

Desmond's eyes widened with pleasant surprise. The second he saw how much his expression amused Margot, he made sure to harden his features, returning to his irritated and suspicious glare.

"Assuming you're telling the truth, you've already helped me, then?"

"I guess I have."

"Okay, then why did you act as if this was something you were *about* to do and not something you've already done?"

"Maybe I minced my words a little," Margot said.

"No. I know the real reason," Desmond said." It's so that I'll be compelled to do a *favour* for you no matter what, isn't it?" he asked.

Margot chuckled in confirmation. Desmond shook his head furiously.

"Contact him and cancel the offer," he insisted. "That deal sounds wonderful, but I don't want to do it if it means I'm indebted to whatever weird bullshit you want me to do."

Margot rolled her eyes. "It's not like I want you to do anything bad. I'd even say you might have some fun doing it," Margot said. "I think you'll *really* like doing it, actually."

Loud alarm bells rang in Desmond's mind as he looked down on her. "What is it?" he sighed.

The corner of Margot's mouth squirmed as she zoned in on him with crazed eyes.

"I want to tell you now, but I'll have to wait and tell you later," she decided with a sigh. "More fun that way."

Margot blew a mocking kiss goodbye to Desmond. She spun around to exit the room. Desmond shook his head as he watched her leave.

As soon as she was out of his sight, Desmond rushed to yank his phone out of his pocket. He opened his email application. To his second surprise, Margot was telling the truth and nothing but the truth. He had received an email from her thirty minutes ago, an email forwarded from Sean

MacGowan, Head Analyst at RealSlaek RF. The same recruiter they were just talking about.

"No way," Desmond scoffed under his breath as he read the email. It confirmed everything Margot had said with further details.

He closed the email and opened his document of notes. It seemed that soon, he would be able to tick one of the unachieved goals. Number #3, have the perfect job lined up. That alone made Desmond smile. A smile that soured once he looked at the final two graduation goals.

He was very unlikely to achieve Number #4 and make lifelong friends. Preferably, he would have as little contact with anyone from this university moving forward. Though he reckoned he would see a lot more of Margot if he ended up working for RealSlaek. Or, if she came to cash in her favour.

Then there was Number #5, which had an even slimmer chance of being realised. To make his parents proud. Proud enough to accept him once again. Proud enough to forgive their last surviving son for all he had done. No matter how prestigious this job was, Desmond had already given up hope that it would be the achievement that would win them over.

If all he had achieved so far was not good enough for them to forgive him, then nothing would be. Perhaps this job would at least take his mind away from that pain.

SOCIALISE, MANIPULATE

GET BACK ON TRACK. Following his newfound job prospects, Desmond was seeking to do exactly that. He had spent the past few months of his life alternating between sinking into the depression hole that was his university flat or aimlessly wandering around his lacklustre hometown in sour solitude. He decided to return to Ivrear following his graduation, but this time with a positive outlook.

He wanted to make some sort of a steady life for himself if he was to take up that Slaek firm position in the next city over. He was not in regular contact with Mr Sean MacGowan of RealSlaek RF, but he had at least received another email setting up an in-person meeting. Until then, he wanted to get himself back into the function of a scheduled life, especially in terms of socialising with others. He had set up a date with a woman from an online dating site, both to brush up on his social skills as well as get used to dating again. It was an afternoon he was very much looking forward to.

***

Desmond left the bar grumbling, having already considered his newfound *stable life* plans to be a waste of time. As he marched down the very same pothole-beggared street next to his neighbourhood that evening, he grunted and seethed over what had been a disappointing afternoon. It was almost as if everything was designed to remind Desmond of the hopelessness of his society and life itself. All of his internal complaints were oriented around Slaek Devices.

The bar he went to had been a dire mess, to say the least. From the second he stepped in, chaos flew in front of his face in the most literal sense. He was almost cut by broken glass that flew across his face, with a plate also scraping past the back of his head. A result of the lack of Slaek Device restrictions within the establishment. Any hedonistic young adult or teen with a Slaek Device could walk in, get drunk, and cause as much havoc with them as their heart desired, floating and throwing miscellaneous items all over the place in inebriated revelry. All he could do was groan as he saw yet another high-schooler pull the same gag of floating a pitcher and dousing their mate with alcohol for the tenth time.

His date herself was one of the worst offenders when it came to Slaek usage. During this date, he had taken the girl he met to a secluded section of the bar, away from the unruly teenagers. It was only a few minutes into the date before he realised it was not going to work out. Whilst he was talking to her, he realised that though she was staring through him, she was not paying attention. She had been using her Slaek Device to float her phone behind his head, facing the screen towards the mirror so she could look past him and read messages. An act that caused Desmond to promptly leave the date and go back downstairs to drink on his own.

But the unequivocal worst user of the Slaek Devices, however, was the one person whom he would have hoped would be the best. In place of employees, the head bartender had fixed one Slaek Device to his right hand and the rest to the walls of the bar, using their magnetic telekinetic properties to take as many orders and dish out as many drinks as possible. Clearly, this was only a recent development of which he was not used to, hence the flying plates and smashed glasses.

Desmond could not last an hour in that *hellscape of an establishment*, as he deemed it. The free time he was supposed to spend enjoying a drink or two with company was instead spent sulking down the road.

***

Desmond decided that he ought not to waste his evening, thinking it would be good to visit his grandmother whilst he was still in town. The only family member he was still on good terms with.

It was getting late and dark. He took a shortcut through a side street to arrive at his destination faster. He wanted to avoid stumbling upon a similar scene to the ones he had witnessed many times before. Yet the very issue he was trying to avoid via the shortcut faced him as soon as he stepped on the cobbled road. A swaying street thug with a gun in one hand and a Roef Device on the other.

"Don't fucking move," the thug ordered, pointing the gun at his head and the arm with the device at his body. Desmond listened, freezing in place. Though his eyes held no fear, his body complied. The thug laughed, flashing an upper row of gold teeth as he took a step closer.

The gold-toothed street thug used his Roef Device to pull apart Desmond's jacket by force. Soon after, he curled his fingers, urging his wallet to release itself from the pocket. Desmond could feel his credit card almost slipping out of his jacket pocket before he was able to zip it up and prevent the theft. He thanked his lucky stars that the thug had not tried to mug him with a proper Slaek Device, or else that credit card would have been appropriated quicker than his eyes could track it floating away from him. He also thanked his lucky stars that at the time, both Slaek and Roef Devices were only capable of controlling and attracting objects towards them and not any form of complex organic matter, such as a human being's body parts. Otherwise, the thug could have forced his hands up and robbed him more efficiently.

"Are you fucking serious right now?" the thug laughed, half-amused, half-indignant. "You looking to get shot or something?"

"No."

"Then open up your jacket and let me take that wallet!"

"I'm not refusing just because I don't want you to rob me. I'm keeping it closed for your sake," Desmond said.

The thug furrowed his slit eyebrows at him. "What the fuck?! Open that jacket now before I kill you!"

"I can't. I have a Slaek Device in the pocket."

"So? Why does that mean shit?!"

"Don't you watch the news? A group of guys got into a shootout with bootleg Slaek Devices involved, and it didn't end well. One had a Roef Device just like yours and accidentally shot himself in the face because the magnetic pull on the other guy's device got all fucked up and yanked the trigger without him wanting to. Curved the bullet into him and everything," Desmond explained as he held his jacket tighter. "It happened on Westout Street, not even a long walk away from here."

"Westout Street?" asked the thug. "Shit, yeah. I think I heard about that."

"Then you *do* realise what will happen if you keep trying to use that Roef Device to pull apart my jacket, don't you?"

Desmond asked. "There's a high chance you end up killing yourself with that gun before you're even able to shoot me."

"Right," the thug agreed, nodding with a pensive glare to the ground. He lowered his gun, raised his head, and briskly walked towards Desmond. "Don't start thinking you talked yourself out of being robbed or something. I'm just gonna take your shit with my bare hands!"

"Fine," Desmond sighed. The thug walked close enough to smell him, thrusting forceful hands towards his body.

As soon as the thug reached for his jacket, Desmond sprang into action. A risky manoeuvre he had planned since the second he decided to tell the thug about the Roef accident. He used the little martial arts he knew to strike the thug's right hand. A quick roundhouse kick to the wrist that, though not powerful enough to injure him, was strong enough to force a drop of the weapon.

"Fucking dickhead!" the thug shouted. He proved to have impressive reflexes, countering with an unavoidable blow of his left fist.

Desmond allowed the punch to strike him in the face, tasting the pooling blood on his tongue as he grabbed the thug's arm. Swift and forceful, he pulled the Roef Device off of his opponent's wrist, leaving a scar. He yanked the thug's arms closer and headbutted him. The thug stumbled backwards, gathering himself as Desmond placed the Roef Device on his wrist.

"Shit!" the thug exclaimed. His eyes darted to the gun as he scrambled towards it with haste.

The second he was set to grab it, the gun floated out of his grasp and into Desmond's curling fingers.

The thug gnashed his golden teeth at Desmond. He growled, then laughed.

"Go on! Shoot it dickhead! That Slaek Device in your pocket's gonna curve that shit straight into your fucking skull!" he gloated.

Desmond shook his head. "I lied. There was no Slaek Device in my pocket, dickhead," he said. "Thought that would have been obvious by now."

The colour seeped from the no longer cocky thug's face. He gulped down a lump in his throat. Desmond smiled.

"Take it easy, bro," the thug pleaded. He raised his hands in surrender.

Desmond's eyes narrowed at the cowering thug. Now that he had the gun in his hand, he was not sure what he was to do. He took a quick glance about his surroundings. No one else in the vicinity. No cameras either. And if his memory served him well, this area was heavily under-policed. Either they would not respond, or they would do so very late and conduct a poorly thought-out investigation. He straightened his back, a shivering heat rising from his gut to his heart to his head. An unshakeable, impulsive instinct.

"No. I don't think I will take it easy, *bro*," Desmond mocked. "When you get to hell, say hello to those Westout Street boys for me, okay?"

The thug ground his teeth. "Don't shoot you fuck-"
Desmond pulled the trigger, aiming for a clean shot through the man's skull. The recoil from the pistol and his lack of experience in aiming a weapon saw it pierce through his neck. Regardless, he succeeded. The thug lay dead, blood leaking from his neck and into the crevices of the cobbled road.

This was the first person that Desmond had killed. Correction, the first person he had killed *intentionally*. He clutched at his swirling stomach. His sealed lips contorted as if he were tasting the blood that leaked from his victim.

Desmond felt another unholy mixture swirling inside his stomach as he sat on an old couch next to his grandmother.

The dull light from the old television shone through the dark room of broken lights and closed blinds. Desmond relaxed on the sofa, almost as still as his dear grandma.

When Desmond first arrived, he had to clean a sore wound that was forming around her wrist from wearing a Slaek Device for too long. It seemed she had forgotten to take it off the previous day, causing an exacerbation of her worsening skin condition. Her eyes were as empty as Desmond's, though in a different manner. One could spend time with her and assume she was brain-dead, with the blank stares and constant silence. She would rarely utter a word to Desmond. It was rare for him to hear her complete a full sentence. When she did, it was some variation of:

"Evelyn, find it in your heart to forgive your son," Mary Bassey would say. "He's a sweet boy. Please forgive him."

Evelyn was the name of her daughter, Desmond's mother. And he, of course, was the sweet boy. Mary's mind had deteriorated over the years, and if ever she was to say something, it would revolve around that.

Later, Desmond ventured on another night walk through his neighbourhood with a new destination in mind. He made his way towards the open yard of a half-burnt-down house at the very end of a cul-de-sac where broken car parts and armless couches rested on the charred grass.

Sitting, standing, and lying around these items were a series of young men similar to the thug he had killed hours ago. Desmond had seen some of the men smoking before he arrived, with one of these individuals bullying another into giving him an extra cigarette by constantly punching him in the ribs until he gave in. This particular man was the blonde-haired, bright-eyed, rough-skinned de facto leader of these thugs. Alistair Armstrong, an unsavoury childhood friend.

"The promised prince has returned!" Alistair cheered. He mockingly bowed down to Desmond, prompting laughs from the other thugs and the man himself.

"Nice to see you again, Alistair," Desmond chuckled. The two hugged, then shook hands.

"You still at uni?"

"Nah, I graduated recently."

"And you came back here? Of all places?"

"Yeah, staying in my old home with my grandma for a bit. Money's tight."

"I get that. But this shithole? Surprised a fine university boy like you didn't force out some extra dosh to move into a better city."

Desmond shrugged. "This will do for the time being." Alistair laughed, rocking Desmond in the ribs with his knuckles. "You just missed being around all the grime and crime, didn't you?" he joked.

"That *is* why I'm here, ironically enough," Desmond said. "I *do* miss it. All the shit we used to do as teens. The parties, the crazy girls, the general chaos. Been a long time since I've had some real fun."

Alistair's smile widened. "I thought you said you've grown out of doing that shit?"

"I'm feeling nostalgic," Desmond chuckled. Alistair spat out the cigarette he had just badgered for.

"You'll get your wish, my friend. The parties, the girls, the insane shit. All of it! Once we're done tonight, you're gonna wish you stayed up in your soft uni city!" Alistair guffawed. The other thugs laughed and cheered in a grunting chorus of rowdy rabbles.

"That's what I like to hear," Desmond said, smiling.

The way he saw it, if society was going to degenerate no matter what, he might as well have some fun and indulge in the degradation.

***

Desmond woke multiple days later, vaguely remembering most of what had happened in the last sixty hours. Wandering eyes and a simple use of context clues pieced everything together. He had woken up in the living room of Alistair's half-burnt-down house, which had been further destroyed by the gang's partying antics. He saw its deterioration continue in real time as pieces of the roof fell and smashed on the floor in clouds of red brick dust.

Over twenty people surrounded him, either sleeping and snoring or resting and groaning as they lay and sat about this post-apocalyptic-esque house. More smashed bottles scattered the floor than at the bar on his date days prior. The walls had either been torn down or stained with booze. He counted at least five broken Roef Devices and three guns from his position to the tile-less kitchen floors. The closest of these twenty-something drunken people was a beautiful curly-haired young lady who had been sleeping right next to him on a dirty camping bag. The two used condoms he found in their sleeping bag filled in the gaps.

Of all the people he saw lying about, Alistair, the person whose house and party it was, was nowhere to be seen. But Desmond had no time to worry about Alistair's whereabouts with much more pertinent issues on his mind.

He checked the date as well as the time. Only a few hours until he was set to have his meeting with Sean MacGowan. He had to get back to his grandmother's house to prepare.

As he ran home, Desmond wondered how a company as prestigious as RealSlaek RF would feel if they knew that one of the top graduates they were head-hunting spent his days partying as if it were the end of the world. He wondered how they would feel if they found out he used a bootleg version of their device to kill a man in a side street days before that.

He put both notions out of his mind. They would not find out about either, he assumed.

MEET, BLACKMAIL

EZRA ELBAZ. Desmond did not follow politics, but even an illiterate child knew the name of Renyland's young president. Especially with all that he had done. Sightings of the president made watching the news a new hobby for him. That morning, in anticipation of his RealSlaek meeting, Desmond flicked through the channels on the television, using them as background noise as he prepared. Once Elbaz's high yet smooth voice could be heard in the background, his interest was piqued. He paid attention to his country leader's appearance on screen.

"...which is why I'm more than happy to announce voyagers from our very own nation have made yet another successful mission back from Planet Ares, making us the first Evincopan country to complete such a voyage twice in a decade!" Elbaz announced, a light shining down on him in the dark newsroom, emphasising the glow of his caramel brown skin and burning-star-white teeth. "I don't see how you can be from this country and not be immensely proud of it. God bless Renyland."

The audience in the studio, wherever Ezra Elbaz was presenting, roared with prideful glory, as did many other

Renyland residents who watched on, Desmond assumed. But he saw no reason to do so himself.

Desmond paused his preparation to stare at Ezra Elbaz. Every time he saw him, he wore the finest-pressed suit and the brightest smile. He had been elected a couple of years ago, where he broke the record for the youngest-ever elected president of Renyland at thirty-five. If his rags-to-riches story was to be believed, he also grew up in an area very similar to Desmond's neighbourhood.

"Say what you want about the man, but he's charming," Desmond thought as he watched him on screen.

He hoped to be half as successful as Ezra Elbaz one day. The first step to achieving such a feat was to attend this RealSlaek RF meeting on time.

***

Half an hour into the meeting, Desmond could not believe how great a time he was having. He had expected to be interviewed and interrogated by a stoic man in a cold office room. Instead, he had been bantering away with the Head Analyst in an Eastern Anrean restaurant as if they were mates.

He laughed and drank over one side of a fluorescent table in a maroon leather booth as Slaek Devices attached to the walls floated plates of eccentrically designed seafood over to them. Desmond loved how, so far, Sean MacGowan was as cordial as they came.

"I would have never guessed you could do that with a shrimp," Sean chortled, the strawberry-blonde formal man almost spilling sauce onto his blazer from the laughter. "Quite the party trick."

"One of the best things I learnt at university," Desmond chuckled as he sipped his drink. The pair enjoyed another few minutes of light discussion and laughter until Sean determined it was time to get straight to business.

"I believe it's time I *cut to the chase*, as people say," Sean said. "Listen. There's a series of recently vacated junior management roles where an analyst needs to lead a team of fellow graduates. We need to replace our ageing team of workers. I want you to fill one of these roles. Can you?"

The light-hearted vibe that had been brought to the table evaporated as Desmond was quickly reminded that this was a serious meeting for an important role. He stopped smiling and started contemplating as he stared back at Sean.

"I'm unsure. I was told by a former classmate of mine that Slaek Device possession and proficiency were not a requirement for the role. Is this right?"

"That's exactly right."

"That's great for me, but is it great for your company? To employ someone at a high level in spite of the fact that they hardly use the product responsible for its success?"

"We want you for your other skills, Eze. Trust me, your role will hardly require in-depth Slaek knowledge or usage."

For some reason, this confirmation failed to fill Desmond with confidence. Without a word or second glance, MacGowan could feel the apprehension radiating off of him.

"You're reluctant to take up the position," Sean noticed, perturbed. "You mentioned having an ill grandmother who you would prefer to be around. Is that the issue? Because if it is, we offer living arrangements for our employees and their family members if need be."

Desmond nodded his head, appreciative of the sweetened offer. Other issues were on his mind, however.

"If I'm to be completely honest, it's not that. I'm more apprehensive about the fact that I will be taking on such a hefty position immediately," Desmond admitted. "It's been many years since I've worked even a part-time job. Probably not the best to admit it, but there's some uncertainty there."

Sean leaned over the table. "Top #10 graduates from Hercole University who studied Analytic Management don't grow on trees, you know," he smirked. "How many times do I have to tell you before you're convinced that you're the right man for the job?"

Desmond sighed. "You're right. I don't get why I'm being so reluctant. This is a fantastic offer I shouldn't even be in the realm of rejecting," he said. "I'll take the role."

Sean backed away with a satisfied smirk, the squeak of leather just as pleasant to his ears as he reclined his back and relaxed in the booth. "Expect to start your work in the next month, Mr Eze."

"Great," Desmond responded with a smile.

***

Another hour later, and the pair were still sitting in their secluded booth at the fancy restaurant.

The cleaned plates of their last seafood course were being whisked off the table by Slaek, clearing the space. With a gesture of his finger, the Slaek Devices floated a laptop over to the table and in front of Sean.

"Would you like to see the last project our firm worked on? To get you familiar with the type of work you'll be doing soon?" he asked as he opened it.

"Yes, please," Desmond said, gesturing at the laptop.

Sean typed, clicked the mousepad, and then turned it around to face Desmond. A video started to play, to which Desmond leaned in and watched attentively.

What had been captured and displayed on MacGowan's laptop was dark to the point that Desmond was not entirely sure of what he was seeing. When he peered closer and saw what had been playing in front of him, he was still not sure.

In it, a group of pale children had been gathered into the corner of a damp stone room. Each of these kids, none older than seven, wore tattered clothes barely sufficient to keep a rodent warm as they quivered in the corner. Twenty seconds into the video, a man with a black eyeless mask and a vantablack suit casually waltzed into the room.

The masked, suited man held a pump shotgun in his hands. He faced the children and used the pump shotgun against them to its full capacity, blasting each one of the poor youth's heads open with a careless pull of the trigger as the next-to-be victims screamed. No discretion was held, each gory detail of the merciless killing of children being captured from all angles. An appalling enough sight to send Desmond speechless for half a minute.

"What the fuck was that?!" he exclaimed at Sean once he found his voice.

"Once you've seen it, you can't unsee it," Sean laughed as he turned the laptop back around.

"What was that?! And why did you show it to me?!" Desmond asked.

"That was a video of one of our employees killing a series of children in order to frame a political faction from the same country we plucked them from," Sean explained as if it was casual and obvious. "Which country? I can't remember. One of the ones with strict regulations against Slaek Device usage in their cities. That's all I know for sure."

Sean's face twisted into a sadistic grin. He chortled incessantly at Desmond's disgusted reaction until his face went as red as his hair.

"Wha-, what the fuck are you saying right now?!" Desmond asked, his voice teetering between rough and angered yet fearful and fragile.

"This is the type of work our top employees do at RealSlaek RF. The type of work you'll be doing very soon," Sean said. Desmond remained speechless.

"The role you're going to fill won't require you to know much about the Slaek Devices our firm produces and distributes, but it will require you to complete certain, shall we say, *unsavoury tasks*, in certain places for certain big investors of ours."

"You want me to do shit like that?!" Desmond asked, pointing a shaky finger at the laptop.

"I won't expect you to do anything of that political scale just yet, but you'll slowly be escalating towards missions of this nature," Sean explained.

"I don't get it. Is this some form of elaborate joke?!" Desmond shouted. "There's not an ice cube's chance in hell I'm doing anything remotely close to that!"

Sean sighed. "You see, the issue is, you will. You most definitely will. You have no other choice in the matter," he said. "This is one of those easy ultimatums. Either you join RealSlaek RF in the capacity I've laid out, or we send the police the evidence we gathered of the murder you committed a few days ago."

Words sharp enough to pierce through Desmond's mind the second he heard them. "What?" he muttered, unsure of what else to say.

"You thought no one saw you shoot that man through the neck just because you saw no cameras or civilians in the general vicinity, didn't you? A novice error. Always triple-check the perimeter before killing a man in public, Mr Eze,"

Sean tutted as if he was scolding a student about a failed exam. "You'll learn that at RealSlaek."

Desmond's typical empty eyes sparkled with life, his pupils dilating as they swelled with fear. His sharp jawline grew sharper as he clenched his teeth together. His chest grew tighter as he struggled for air.

"You know, I'm very grateful you decided to intentionally kill that useless thief in public. Before you did, I planned to threaten to expose you for that incident where you accidentally killed your siblings. You know, the incident your parents never forgave you for?" Sean mocked, as cruel as ever. "But this is simpler blackmail, which always works better. Much cleaner. Straightforward."

Desmond could not keep himself upright, degenerating into a catatonic state of despondency. A shock to the mind that drained into the body and threatened to cause him to pass out. He struggled to digest all that had been thrown at him. Was this real? How did RealSlaek know all this information about him? What was going to happen to him now?

Sean's stifled smile broke out again. "As I said before, a bunch of crucial roles in this *sector* have been vacated. People who either died during their missions or fled from the company in a desperate attempt to escape their duties. Though if you do the latter, you'll end up as the former. Obviously," the redhead laughed.

Desmond scoffed at him. "All this time," he muttered, shaking his head as he lowered his eyes. "This is what you've been head-hunting me for? All this time?"

"Can you blame us? You fit the profile for our ideal employee."

"What profile?"

30

Sean leaned over the table again. With a big smirk and dancing eyes, he lifted three fingers.

"Clever, capable of cruelty, and compromised."

WORRY, MASSACRE

REALSLAEK RF. Desmond was officially an employee of the prestigious tech firm, the greatest manufacturer and distributor of the most revolutionary technology of the '20s.

Days following their meeting, Desmond remained in his shell-shocked state. He woke up every day half-convinced that what had happened was a nightmare he had escaped from, only for reality to make itself known. He remembered how Sean MacGowan defined the work of his division:

Completing certain unsavoury tasks, in certain places, for certain big investors.

Based on the video of the children being killed, that definition was an understatement. A sugar-coating.

Desmond could not fathom the fact that he was expected to partake in such missions with other graduates. Though he accepted that he would have to. He truly had no choice in the matter. If he did not, he would either be exposed for the murder he committed or be murdered himself. Either way, there was no hope for an occupation change in his future. He was a RealSlaek employee for the rest of his life. However long that would be. Desmond had a whole lot to think of, though barely enough time to think it. It was soon time for him to complete his very first *unsavoury mission.*

***

Since Desmond's last visit during the raging party, Alistair had major repairs done to his home. Major improvements by his standards, at least. The hole in the roof had been patched up with plaster, the section of the east side of the house that had been crumbling was brought down in its entirety, and new car parts, old sofas, and mattresses were placed out front for him and his gang to mill about on. Desmond sat by Alistair himself as he and his mates, or *the hoodlums* as they were often called, went through their most important daily task. Smoking the afternoon away.

One of the hoodlums, a lanky man with track marks on his arms, took a cigarette out of his mouth between his fingers and tapped Alistair on the shoulder. "We still on for the party tonight?" he asked.

"Ah, right, the party. Forgot we were having another tonight," Alistair said as he sat up. He nudged Desmond on the side, who was mindlessly sinking into his chair. The only person on the porch who was not holding a cigarette. "You up for a party tonight?"

"Sure," Desmond said nonchalantly.

"If Des is up for it, I'm up for it. We'll host it here again," Alistair said.

The lanky man nodded as if to say *cool* without doing so. A tattooed hoodlum stood up off the couch, eyebrows furrowed, looking as if he had something important to add.

"Is it alright if the Greene brothers come?" he asked.
The track-marked hoodlum immediately scoffed with derision. "The fucking Greene brothers? You better be having a laugh!" he yelled.

33

"Come on, they're my boys!" the tattooed hoodlum said.

"Your boys who almost blew up my car with fireworks last party we invited them to!" the track-marked hoodlum complained.

"They'll act right," the tattooed hoodlum assured.

"You better fucking make sure they do," Alistair threatened as he pointed a cigarette his way. "Or both you and them will end up wrecked worse than that car was."

The tattooed hoodlum nodded again. Desmond knew that the hoodlum knew that Alistair was not making empty threats. Alongside one of the tattoos on his arm was a faint, wide scar from the last threat Alistair followed through on.

As Alistair and the hoodlums continued to talk and smoke, Desmond sat up silently on the rough porch sofa. His heart sped up, beating with enough force to implode itself as he thought about this party that was to take place that evening. It was to be the grounds where he would complete his first covert mission on behalf of RealSlaek RF.

***

As the sky darkened and night fell, the party went underway. An outdoor function took place in which hoodlums and street girls congregated around the general vicinity of Alistair's house at the end of the cul-de-sac.

With bottles of beer and spirits in each of their hands, the party attendees were great enough to fill that area from the side of Alistair's house where Desmond and the hoodlums started hanging out, all the way to the end of the street that made up that section of the neighbourhood.

Desmond sat by a kerb on his own, nursing his half-drunk bottle of cognac. He could see Alistair at the other end of the neighbourhood, gyrating in an aggressive dance routine as two scantily-clad women danced with him, shaking their backsides against his crotch with their tongues stuck out. Even if Desmond wanted to, he could not join him. Nor could he join the others in the main thoroughfare of the party. He kept his distance, panicking internally as he thought of how he was to carry out this RealSlaek mission.

Sean MacGowan gave Desmond no instructions when it came to what he was to do other than the following three points. 1 - The mission was to be completed in a low-income neighbourhood in his area. 2 - To complete it, he was given a small but powerful temporary Slaek Device that was currently hidden around his arm underneath his long-sleeve shirt and jacket. And 3 - That he was to use both the device and his environment to create a *newsworthy massacre of greatly eye-catching proportions.* He was not even told how this would help RealSlaek or their big investors, just that he ought to do it. He felt dehydrated, assuming this was a result of the immense amount of sweat leaving his body from the mixture of the alcohol he had drunk, the layers he wore to conceal his Slaek, and the nerve-wracking prospect that was succeeding in this mission.

"How am I going to do this?" he muttered, shaking.

***

"Desmond, man! Get off that fucking kerb and join the festivities!" Alistair shouted over at him from the other end of the neighbourhood. He boomed his message through a police microphone as he danced by a crowd of people who cheered him on. A piece of equipment that Desmond knew they had not obtained legally.

"Nah, I'm good!" Desmond shouted back, rejecting the offer with a shake of his head and a crossing motion against his neck. Alistair scoffed at Desmond, mocking his rejecting gesture. He threw the police microphone on the floor and threw himself back into the dancing crowd.

Desmond remained on his lonesome by the kerb, his bottle of cognac empty as he stressed over his task. He considered the prospect of not doing the mission at all.

Intentionally cause a massacre? In his own city? In his own neighbourhood? The thought alone was many levels beyond sickening. But he had to be honest with himself. Not completing it was not an option.

Commit a great murder, be exposed for murder, or be murdered himself. He felt bad admitting it, but the first option was the one he had to choose. Sean MacGowan was another man capable of carrying out his threats.

Desmond needed to at least make sure Alistair was not one of the victims caught in the crossfire if he was to make the eye-catching, newsworthy spectacle. If he was going to murder people from his own area, he had to at least make sure his childhood mate went unscathed. Could he control for that, though? Too many variables to consider and not a single inkling of an idea of execution.

As Desmond clutched at his pounding head with the empty bottle in hand, the cruellest of miracles was performed in front of him. He had heard the sounds of dancing and cheering die down by a considerable amount, being replaced by a different, much more concerning rise of noise. He looked across the street where he stood to see a great number of hoodlums and street girls engaged in aggressive, belligerent shouting matches as they screamed over one another. He could not make out how the disagreement started, but he could make out that two young male thugs were at the heart of the conflict in the middle of the crowd.

"You looking to die?!" asked one hoodlum, placing a hand on the gun at his hip.

"The fuck did you just say?!" the other shouted back, pulling out a pistol of his own from the back of his trousers.

Both men pointed their guns at each other, building panic and aggression in the air as the crowd threw themselves at each other with greater ferocity. The potent concoction of frightened yet hostile spirits leaked through the streets until the whole party was involved in the conflict.

This was the perfect opportunity. All Desmond had to do was find a way to exacerbate the already tense and violent atmosphere, building it up to a gunfight and thus a massacre. A plan was formed in an instant.

The men and women of lower-class persuasions who gathered to party that evening all attempted to either mitigate or aggravate the situation. Both efforts caused the tension to rise. Both gun-wielding hoodlums were reaching their limit.

"Take that fucking gun out of my f-"

All who had gathered witnessed the first kill of the night. A bullet flew forward, making the hoodlum's last words an incomplete sentence. A bloody plump hole was made through his lower mouth and across his forehead.

The aggressor who fired the shot's eyes darted from the gun to his fallen victim. Despite his blatant pointing of the pistol in the other's face, he wore a look of despairing shock, as if the kill had been a complete accident.

The crowd exploded into screams. Members of the party began to desperately flee, whilst others saw this as an opportunity to add to the chaos, pulling out their guns in defence. One shot fired, and the entire neighbourhood was on edge. The situation was soon to worsen. As the dead man's body hit the floor, the gun fell from his hand, rattling on the floor. Once the gun stilled, those surrounding the body saw the weapon do the impossible.

The trigger had been accidentally activated, with a bullet launching itself out of the barrel and in between the eyebrows of the closest person to it. As the bullet exited the back of the dead woman's head, it found its way into the head of another. The same happened once more, this one bullet seeming to curve and lodge itself in the neck of a male victim, and shortly after, the chest of a fourth.

"What the fuck is going on!" screamed one of the street girls, tears pouring from her eyes and blood down her face as her sentiments echoed throughout the neighbourhood.

Even the most aggressive of partygoers decided to cut their losses in a frantic panic and dash as far away from the street as they could manage.

A quarter of all the gun owners who had brought out their pieces in defence sorely regretted it. Each of them succumbed to the fate of a curved bullet that, after killing them, dispatched others in their vicinity. The entire estate rang with a concurrent chorus of screams of blood, tears of woe, and the thuds and smacks of over twenty bullet-ridden bodies.

Desmond hid himself behind Alistair's house, the position he had fled to as soon as shots were fired. Only once he made sure Alistair had fled the scene did he step out of cover. He winced in pain, gripping his jacket as he clasped the powerfully surging Slaek Device attached to his arm, giving his skin a light burn underneath.

Unbeknownst to a single other soul there that night, this had all been his doing.

* * *

Desmond had reached a perpetual state of emotional severance. A month prior, he could have confidently said he never intentionally caused grievous bodily harm to a fellow human being. Now, he held a higher body count than the average modern-day serial killer and caused enough death and destruction to be labelled as a domestic terrorist. Following the massacre he created, Desmond did not worry or fret over the evil committed. Not out of a tempered remorse or rationalising of his actions, but out of a conscious effort on his part to ignore its very existence in order to maintain his sanity.

As quiet as a dull child, Desmond mindlessly followed Sean MacGowan up the stairs of a building they had entered from a dark secret passageway in an abandoned side street in Capcounty City. As he climbed each step, he could tell from the gold and maroon colour pattern of the railings and walls, as well as floral designs on the stair carpeting, that they were in some form of inner-city hotel complex. When they reached the top of the stairs, all that was available to them was a landing and a singular door to a room. Desmond realised every room in this complex must have had its own designated section. An impressive feat for any establishment. He would never see this in an Ivrear hotel.

Sean slung a key out of his pocket, swiftly placing it in the hole and twisting it unlocked. "Welcome to your new home," he said, swinging the door open with pomp and flair.

Desmond's eyes took a quick overview of his new place of stay. It was, without a doubt, the nicest living space he ever had the privilege of owning. The front area of a simple cream-coloured apartment with a television large enough to cover the surface area of the entire wall, a living room that would dwarf most homes in his hometown, and a RealSlaek RF care package waiting for him on the kitchen island.

"Thank you," Desmond uttered, unbothered.

A while ago, if he had been told this was to be his new permanent home, he would have thought he was being blessed beyond reasonable measures. The thought of what he had to do in order to receive it sullied what would have been a moment of emotional gratitude.

"Your grandmother has been moved to a similar room a few buildings over for employee family members. She's got many of our best carers staying with her. We'll get a key made for you, too."

Desmond nodded, avoiding contact with Sean's reptilian eyes as the analyst placed a hand on his shoulder.

"I need to ask you an important question, Sean."

"If it's to do with the apartment, then wait, I've not finished explaining everything to you yet."

"It's about the mission I completed."

Sean's reptilian expression grew more unnerving, his eyes slimming as his mouth tightened into a closed grin. "Yes?"

"What was its purpose?" Desmond asked, his emotionless voice speckled with the curious tone of a student.

"Does your generation not keep up with the news anymore, Mr Eze?"

"I do usually, but I've been intentionally avoiding it recently. Because of the mission."

Sean laughed, tilting his head back as he opened up his suit blazer. He reached into a side pocket, pulling out a foldable electronic tablet. He turned it on, swiped a few times, then turned it towards Desmond.

"Give that a good glance and a gander," Sean ordered as he shoved the tablet into his hands.

Desmond read the news article. "Tragedy at Ivrear neighbourhood slum. A score of young men and women are killed in a gunfight turned massacre."

He kept reading. The general gist of the article was that an altercation in a *slum* led to guns being drawn. The article went on to mention the strange phenomenon of curving bullets that killed multiple targets, blaming this bizarre occurrence on a malfunction caused by the Roef Devices that were 'found' around the neighbourhood following the fallout, as opposed to the Slaek Device that had caused a day-long searing burn on Desmond's arm. All this information was exactly what Desmond expected to see. But he could not yet figure out the true purpose of the mission.

He read a series of quotes from celebrities, politicians, and influential people of Renyland giving their two cents on the massacre. Most said something along the lines of how awful a tragedy it was and how such an unfortunate incident would not have occurred if the people of this *Ivrear slum* did not have to resort to using the bootleg Slaek Devices that were flooded into their neighbourhoods.

The quotes that interested him the most were the thoughts given by President Ezra Elbaz. He echoed the sentiments of the other influential figures whilst adding promises to rectify this issue. He vowed to fix both the pervasiveness of the Roef problem with the issues of the inner city, proposing a scheme to create small towns of tight-knit communities that ran on a *shared Slaek-Grid*. A proposal for a grand-scale living arrangement, in which he hoped everyone would be living in some form of by the late 2020s. The *Slaek-City*.

If this story had succeeded in doing anything, it was increasing the demand for higher-quality Slaek Devices to be made and distributed in Ivrear, which would undoubtedly benefit the pockets of their top distributor, RSRF.

Desmond also realised the secondary purpose of the mission. To test his capabilities, to test his will to kill, and to create another blackmail story should he choose not to return for another mission. He scoffed, gesturing at Sean to take the device away from him.

"You're beginning to get a clear picture of what we're about here at RealSlaek, aren't you, Eze?" Sean chuckled as he took the tablet back out of his hands.

"Yes," Desmond sighed. "I am."

INTRODUCE, INTEGRATE

THE HOTEL. No official name. That was all it was known as. *The Hotel*. A large building of plain, cream interiors where all employees of this particular division of RealSlaek lived. All under one gigantic roof, where they could do as they pleased with minimal supervision until they were to be activated for more unscrupulous missions.

Desmond sat on a sofa by a plant in the hotel lobby, a few paces away from the reception desk. He watched other graduates, just like him, check themselves in with the help of receptionists booking them in, and bellhops using Slaek Devices to float their luggage to its desired location. He had been to similar hotels like this one in the past and seen similar employees and patrons. All looked as unassuming as the RSRF employees he saw around him that day. Had he been a civilian teleported into this lobby, there was no way to tell what these genial men and women were truly capable of.

"Morning, Desmond!" one of his female coworkers cheerfully greeted as she walked by.

"Morning, Izzy," Desmond greeted back.

A couple of weeks had passed since he completed his first mission and moved into his apartment. He was friendly with a great number of other employees by this point, having eased himself into the daily routine of RSRF work.

The previous day, he was sent on a mission that, although low-level, still possessed the firm's gruesome flair. He journeyed to the house of a man to cover up his death. An elderly man who had no friends or family left to speak of and relied on Slaek Devices to feed and clean himself until they broke down one day. Desmond was tasked with cleaning the man's body and destroying any proof of him ever owning a Slaek Device to cover that the elderly distress function was ignored, making sure no blame could be traced back to RSRF.

Thinking of that mission inspired him to visit and care for his grandmother some more.

***

"Aren't you the sweetest boy?" Grandma Mary kept reiterating in delirium as Desmond helped her get underneath the ivory-coloured pressed bedsheets in her company-provided apartment room.

"Thanks, grandma," Desmond said as he tucked her in.

"Have you and your mother made up yet?" she asked him, rather talkative that day.

"Not yet, grandma," Desmond told her.

"Oh," she sighed with disappointment. "Promise me you'll try speaking to her today, okay?"

"I will," Desmond assured, despite having not made any efforts to speak to her recently and not planning on contacting her anytime soon.

With all the new information he had to process with RealSlaek, he had not even thought about his parents. The last time the thought of his mother crossed his mind was during his meeting at the restaurant with Sean MacGowan. When the head RealSlaek employee revealed the company

44

knew about his actions that led to the accidental death of his siblings and were planning to use that story as blackmail before they discovered he killed that thug. Even then, his mind was less focused on the incident itself and his parents' persistent distaste for him because of it, and more so on how the company were able to find such information. Had they contacted his parents themselves, or were they just that good at digging? Whichever was the case, it concerned him.

Later, Desmond sat on the couch of his grandmother's apartment after she finished her lunch and went to sleep. He wore a blazer and jeans in a similar style to Sean MacGowan and multiple other male employees. He held in his hands the same brand of foldable company tablet and scrolled through his itinerary. A bland, boring online timetable that, aside from the rare real-time flicker on the screen to indicate a change of schedule, was not much to look at. All the items on the timetable were boring two-word pieces of information, such as 'Clean Up', 'Inventory Check', 'Market Research' and 'Company Liaison'. They were code words for missions he had to memorise. From what he had learned thus far, 'Market Research' usually meant "You will either be carrying out a killing or overseeing another employee doing so."

That afternoon, he spotted a new code he had never come across before. 'Integration Time'. He did a little research and a lot of asking around to find out this was the code name for a simple party. An event for the new recruits to enjoy the fruits of their good work so far.

***

Desmond dressed himself in a finer blazer and sleeker black jeans. He was escorted into a great hall on the third lowest floor of The Hotel. The room had a smooth yet eerie ambience to it with a mixture of classical music and slowed-down modern pop tunes playing in the background. All members of the company around Desmond's age, fellow graduates presumably, mingled around the tables and chairs, with Slaek Devices acting as their personal waiters as they drank and ate. A Slaek Device next to him triggered, automatically floating a small bowl of shrimp rice and a small bottle of cognac into his hands. The same meal choice he had made at the meeting with MacGowan.

"Hilarious," Desmond scoffed at the not-so-subtle joke as he caught both food items. He ate the portion of rice and made progress with the cognac as he sat down on the first empty seat he found.

After a few minutes of eating and drinking on his own, he thought he might as well treat this as the party it was and talk to the other well-dressed young employees around him. He stared at another bottle of cognac, which prompted whoever or whatever was controlling the Slaek Devices around the area to float two over, one into his hands and another into his blazer pocket.

"Nice," Desmond muttered. He opened one, took a sip, and looked for a group of workers to mingle with. He spotted a mixed group of men and women by a stone fountain.

"Hey, how are you guys doing?" he greeted after approaching them. "I'm Desmond."

"Nice to meet you, Desmond," one of the girls in the group said, immediately turning to him.

Again, he was caught off guard by the geniality of the average employee here. The rest greeted him with bright smiles and enthusiastic waves, opening up a space for him to join their group discussion. Desmond smiled, relaxing as he took another big swig of his drink.

"We were just talking about how great the perks here are. I got a coupon for unlimited free drinks for two bars in the city centre!" one of the men in the group celebrated.

"Yeah, I was just thinking about that," Desmond said. "The Slaek Devices they've got here are higher quality than any I've ever seen. And the apartment rooms without rent? It's still hard to believe we get all these extras for free."

"I wouldn't say for free," one of the other guys laughed ominously. "We all have to pay a price for this job."

Each member of the group laughed along with them, picking up what he had been putting down. It took Desmond a brief second to understand. Each and every one of these people was a new recruit straight out of university, just like him. They had all been blackmailed and made to create a *newsworthy spectacle*. They seemed to be coping with it better than he was. Desmond laughed awkwardly with them, instinctively taking another swig.

He did not know if it was the alcohol talking, but he came to a surprising conclusion. Instead of moping about as he had been in his first few weeks, he should try his hardest to make the best life possible for himself whilst he was here. Instead of going through the motions, he should build himself. He should truly integrate into the culture of RealSlaek, just as he was doing now, but also when sober and at all times.

That was the only way he could see himself coping with this insane job. The first step to that was to make as many friends at this event as he possibly could.

***

Desmond felt as if he were his friend Alistair at a neighbourhood block function. He effectively made himself the life of the party after a couple of hours and a lot of drinks later in the evening.

"Sink them! Sink them! Sink them!" the group Desmond joined cheered as he completed a drinking challenge. Slaek Devices floated two small bottles of almond liquor and a heavy cherry vodka above his head, draining them into his mouth until both were finished. Once both bottles were empty, the Slaek Devices stopped floating them, allowing Desmond to catch both in his hands and let out a triumphant roar as the group around him celebrated his achievement.

Drunker, happier, and more willing to let loose, the integration event between the recent-graduate employees was going well. By that point in the night, Desmond no longer felt as if he was at a company event. He felt as if he was back at university or attending a house party or on the block with Alistair, the hoodlums, and street girls.

Desmond sat in a circle of chairs, taking a break from the dancing and drinking, alongside a couple of the guys he had come to know throughout the night.

"I never would have expected a Hercole University graduate to be this cool," said Jack, a bearded workmate, in between his efforts to down a bottle of beer.

"Weren't all of us here recruited from top-tier universities?" Desmond asked him, laughing.

"Yeah, we were. But I'm a Top #20 graduate from Rencrown, where people know how to party," Jack stated. "Unlike the stuffy Hercole students I've met. Surprised you weren't like those humourless bastards."

"I'm glad to have surprised you," Desmond chuckled.
They enjoyed each other's company as they people-watched. Desmond took note of the dresses some of the young women were wearing. Almost all of them with designs that fit their forms near-perfectly. There was a stirring within him.

"You got your eyes on any ladies tonight?" Jack asked.

"Did you read my mind?" Desmond asked.

"Wouldn't have to. Your eyes have been floating around the girls around here like they had Slaek installed in them."

"I'm being that obvious?"

"You are. Have you not been with a woman in a while?"

"Not any that are quality."

"How's that? You're a good-looking guy. You telling me no girls are trying for you?"

Desmond sighed. "It's because of other reasons. Reasons I'm only starting to get over now," he stated. "Probably why my eyes seem to be floating over every girl."

"Even a guy who looks like you can't have all of them. Who are you going for in particular?" Jack questioned.

Desmond narrowed his gaze and swivelled his head. He assessed all of the young women around the hall who had captured his interest. A few had piqued this interest the most, but one stood head and shoulders above the rest. Unequivocally.

"Her," Desmond decided with a wry smile. He set his sights on a short, brown-skinned young woman with big hazel eyes and a voluptuous figure that made an infinite number of carnal thoughts pass through his mind. He finally understood what people meant when they spouted cliches about smiles that lit up rooms. Because hers was radiant. Whatever she was talking about with her group of friends, they seemed as entranced by her as he was. A smile that saw him pre-emptively planning a hypothetical family life. "Definitely her."

Once Jack saw who he was referring to, an even wryer smile crept across his face. "Chantelle Belle? That's who you want to pull?" he scoffed.

"Why? What's wrong with her?"

"Nothing, man. I just don't think it's a good decision for you to try it with her."

"Is this a '*she's out of your league*' thing?"

"Not really. She *is*, but only a little."

"Then what's the problem?"

Jack leaned back in his chair, tilting his head closer to Desmond as the two stared at her. "She is one of the most beautiful girls in our RealSlaek generation, yet I've seen barely any guys approach her after her first day here. Even though they approach all of her friends and girls less gorgeous than her all the time. And when I've asked them why, none of those few guys can give me a straight answer. Why do you think that is?"

"No idea," Desmond answered.

"Exactly. Doesn't that alarm you a little?" Jack asked.

Desmond nodded. "You're saying there might be something wrong with her that we don't know yet? Something those few guys are too afraid to tell the rest of us about?"

"Basically," Jack sighed. "I'm telling you, man, you're going to become a cautionary tale if you do end up pulling her. I'd hate for you to-"

Before Jack had even finished his explanations, Desmond stopped listening and started approaching her, the courage of alcohol spurring him onwards. Chantelle had departed from her group of friends for a moment as she eyed the bottled drinks selection at the end of a grand table, freeing her up for Desmond to talk to. He saw this as a sign from the universe that he was right to have approached her, regardless of Jack's warnings.

"Chantelle, is it?" Desmond asked as he stood by her. She pivoted towards him, greeting him with a pleasant smile.

"It is. Chantelle Belle," she said.

"Desmond Eze," he replied with a firm offer of a handshake, which she softly accepted.

"Mr Eze," she said. It sounded a lot more endearing out of her mouth than when Sean MacGowan condescendingly referred to him in the same manner.

"I've heard quite a few people mention you here. The way they talk, you'd think you were the most beautiful girl alive," Desmond said, smiling as he blatantly checked her out. "I wouldn't go quite as far as agreeing, but I can see where they're coming from, if only a little."

Chantelle scoffed, finding him both bold and amusing. "You're alright looking yourself," she said, giving Desmond the type of smirk that made him more confident about this being the right move.

"According to my friend over there, flirting with you is asking for trouble," he said.

"Me? Trouble?" Chantelle laughed.

"Apparently so," Desmond chuckled. "Apparently, for some reason, I'm one of the few guys who is still willing to risk approaching you."

"That's funny, I don't see why. I'm harmless."

"You're definitely not, Chantelle."

"I'm not?"

Desmond locked eyes with her in a deep gaze. "Everyone here's just started working for RSRF's mission division," Desmond said, his head vaguely gesturing at the party around them as he mischievously smiled. "Not a single one of us is harmless. We're all far from it. Especially me."

This statement seemed to entice Chantelle far more than Desmond had even intended. She let a deep breath out of her nose as she closed the distance between them. She laid a gentle hand on his shoulder.

"You want to know why no other guy wants to take the risk of trying to get with me?" Chantelle whispered, sultry.

"I do," Desmond whispered back. Chantelle chuckled with menace.

"If I tell you, there's a decent chance I will have to kill you at some point in the future," she said, her eyes flirtatious yet her tone deadpan and serious. "And that isn't some kind of snarky joke. It's a genuine possibility."

Desmond's heart skipped a beat, a touch of fear interfering with the supreme confidence the alcohol was granting him. He maintained composure despite what sounded like a threat to him.

Any other type of woman in any other type of place, and this would have been an obvious line of light-hearted banter. But at RealSlaek RF, it was a different story. He decided the best response was to treat it as if it were a snarky joke.

"This job itself, knowing what this company *really* does, puts my life in constant danger," he said. "I might as well learn another dangerous secret whilst I'm at it."

Chantelle drew herself back. She placed both hands behind her back, looking up to him as if she were a dainty princess. "Would you like to have a private drink with me, Desmond?"

"Only if you'd like to have a private drink with me," Desmond chuckled. Chantelle smirked.

***

Hours later, the party was winding down to a close. Many of the recent graduates, especially the group Desmond had been acquainted with, had fallen into drunken stupor. Fresh-faced RSRF employees slung themselves across the floors and chairs as the music died down. They drank and ate the last morsels of food and alcohol that were being floated around.

"Where's that Desmond guy gone? He was funny!" a short male coworker asked Jack.

"Last I saw of him, he left to go down the hall with that Chantelle girl," Jack said, gesturing towards the corridors at the end of the hall. They led beyond the wine cellars and towards private rooms.

"He left the party with Chantelle Belle?!" the short coworker gasped as if he had been told someone was performing a miracle.

"I know, right? Impressive," Jack commented.

"That guy's a different breed," the coworker sighed as he looked down the hall.

***

Chantelle lay on top of Desmond on the bed in a dark room. The pair kissed, passionate and fervid yet smooth and gentle as they explored each other's bodies with their hands. They moved with fluid sexual synchronicity, ready to make their two forms one as they slowly undone their clothes. As Desmond reached to unclip the back of her bra, however, Chantelle broke their embrace. She unlocked her lips from his and stared at him with wondering eyes.

"Didn't you want to know about my secret? The one that makes guys wary about trying to seduce me?" she asked him. "Has a kiss and a fondle made you forget?"

"I assumed you would tell me *after* we were done," Desmond laughed.

Chantelle rolled her eyes. She dismounted him, breaking full contact as she sat to the side of the bed.

"If we're going to go any further than we already have, you'll have to know about my secret," she seemed to decide on a whim.

"Tell me," Desmond urged.

53

Chantelle paused for a while. "It's to do with my parents."

"What about them?" Desmond asked.

Chantelle paused again. For the first time since they had met hours earlier, she avoided eye contact. She took up a softer, more vulnerable disposition as she stared into the black space to the side of her.

"When I get with a guy, it's never a short-term thing. I won't have sex with you until I'm ready to tell you. And I won't be ready to tell you unless you plan on making me your girlfriend," she said. A proposal Desmond did not expect, but was not put off by.

Desmond stretched his neck to the side to crack it. He considered the proposal for a moment before answering.

"I'm fine with things heading in that direction," he determined. From the look on Chantelle's face, such acceptance was a surprise.

"You'll be fine with us getting to know each other for a while before we do anything?" she asked.

"Yeah," Desmond answered, shrugging.

"Wonderful," she said, that room-brightening smile of hers returning. She zipped her dress, closing the window of opportunity for sex that night.

Desmond sighed.

***

Later, Desmond found himself a touch sexually frustrated. Though he reasoned that in the long run, this was a more positive experience for him. A potential one-night stand turned into a potential relationship. The thought of seeing Chantelle again fuelled him with the same excitement he had when he had first approached her. Everything about her intrigued him. Especially whatever the secret about her parents was.

Desmond wondered whether agreeing to date her was getting himself into more trouble than was worthwhile.

FAVOUR, SETTLE

A GOOD LIFE. That was all Desmond ever wanted. To live the type of life others could look towards with pride and envy, the type they would have no other choice but to either emulate, or desperately try to. After his first two months at RSRF, it looked as if he was on the fast-road to achieving that. He was becoming much more well-known and well-liked at the firm, especially amongst those in his division and the other recent graduates he fraternised with. He had come to terms with the seedy nature of his secret Slaek work with their help and chosen to focus more on the high pay and constant perks it gave him. And he was dating Chantelle Belle, a girl who, so far, was as wonderfully kind and sweet as they came.

Desmond whistled to himself contentedly as he wiped down his kitchen's countertop until it was spotless. He was in the best mood he had been in years. The previous night, Chantelle had given him a surprise. She had initially stated they would not have sex until she was ready to tell him the secret about her parents that made others wary of her, but the previous night, she could not contain herself. Desmond ended up having the best sex he had ever had that night, with the most beautiful woman he had ever been with. Afterwards, as they had lain in bed, he assumed Chantelle would finally reveal the secret. Yet it did not come up. Not once.

He wondered as to why it had not, but chose not to tempt ruining a great thing and kept quiet on the matter. If she wanted to tell him, she would have. He also reasoned that if it was a truly horrible secret, even if she ended up refusing to tell him, he would find out. Things of that nature always had a habit of revealing themselves. When the time came, he would handle it.

Desmond heard a soft, dainty knocking on his apartment door. With a cheesy grin, he left the kitchen to answer it, expecting Chantelle on the other side when he opened the door. He was instead faced with a different woman he knew. One whom he had forgotten about over the past two months, and if it was up to him, would have kept it that way.

Margot Forster cheekily grinned at him as she twirled a thick strand of her dark brown hair. "It's been a while since we've seen each other, Des," she laughed.

"It hasn't been long enough," Desmond scoffed, scowling at her.

He had put Margot out of his mind for such a long time that only in that moment did he consciously remind himself she was the reason he had the blackmailing restaurant meeting with Sean MacGowan in the first place. He now associated his frustration during that event with her presence.

Margot slinked past Desmond, waltzing into the apartment. Her eyes spanned all over the interior as she walked further in. She sat herself on the plush sofa, stretching out her arms and legs as if this were her home. Desmond walked over, glaring at her from the other side of a glass coffee table.

"Look at all the nice company stuff you got, Eze. All because I set up that meeting for you! I hope you haven't forgotten I'm the reason you're here?"

"I've been busy. You've barely crossed my mind," Desmond said. "And I've not seen you around, so I forgot you worked for this company. Didn't realise how many other divisions all over the country there were."

"Who said I worked in any division?"

"Why else would you have gotten me this job if you didn't work here?"

"You're right, I do work here, but not in this division," Margot said. "Not until two weeks ago."

"You switched divisions?" asked Desmond, not realising that was a choice. "Why?"

"This is the division with the most lucrative opportunities," Margot explained. "It's also the division where I can get as close to you as possible."

Margot smiled in a manner that caused Desmond discomfort. He crossed his arms.

"Is this about the favour I still owe you?"

"It is."

"Go ahead and say it. I'll see if I can do it."

"Surely you're not considering abandoning your promise, Desmond?"

"I'm still considering if I should even let you talk."

Margot laughed. "Alright, I need you to let me live in this apartment for the next few weeks. Maybe a little longer," she stated. "Don't ask why, it's part of the favour."

Let a strange former classmate of his live in his home for a short while, yet not ask any questions about it? It was a favour that sounded as innocuous as it was shady.

"No."

"No?!"

"You're not living here until you give me the reason why you need to," Desmond scoffed.

"I'll ask again. You're not considering abandoning your promise, are you, Desmond?" Margot asked.

"Explain exactly why you're doing this. Explain whatever you're planning from A to Z, or else I'm not letting you," Desmond insisted.

Margot groaned. She glared Desmond in the eye, realising it would take more effort than it was worth to keep him from prying.

She whipped out her phone and clicked on an application that gave her a live video feed of her apartment. She gestured for him to come watch it with her. Margot's apartment looked very similar to Desmond's. If he had decided to turn it into a drug den, that is. Powders, pills, cardboard packages, and people in white T-Shirts populated the space as they cut, syphoned, wrapped, packaged and at times, openly ingested the product all over the tables.

"A little project I'm working on. Got in contact with a girl I used to date in the inner-city who helped swindle some stupid thugs out of the keys to a safehouse. I'm using my apartment as the main place of production because it's easier to retrieve the Slaek Devices we need to distribute them contactless from company grounds," Margot explained with a giddy smile. "We're going to flood the slums of this city with our product in the most efficient way fucking possible!"

"Is this part of a mission you're doing for the division?" Desmond asked. He imagined a scheme of flooding the slums of the city with drugs and utilising Slaek Devices for efficiency to be the *exact* type of plan the firm would come up with for a mission. But Margot shook her head.

"The opposite. What I'm doing is against employee rules. That's why I've hired a few hackers throughout the company to manipulate the camera feeds around my parts. And it's also why I have set the room to explode and burn in a 'random Slaek malfunctioning accident' the second we get caught, if we do," Margot explained further, even giddier than before. "I don't want to be anywhere near the place in case that happens. Plus, it's hard to sleep with the smell of cannabis and coke wafting through the apartment air all the time."

"Jesus Christ," Desmond sighed, shaking his head. A plan as hare-brained as this was exactly the type of insane scenario a woman like Margot Forster would be involved in.

"So, can I stay at yours for a few weeks? As a return of my favour?" she asked.

"Yes, a favour's a favour. But you'll have to sleep in the back room and make yourself scarce. In fact, try not to leave it as much as possible when you're here. Especially when I have company," he said.

"Why's that?"

"I'm dating someone right now. I don't think she'll be particularly happy if she finds out another woman is sleeping in my apartment."

Margot giggled. "That makes this whole thing a whole lot more interesting."

"Don't make me take back the favour," Desmond threatened. "Agree to those terms right now. Promise you will make yourself scarce."

"Trust me, I will. For your sake, not mine," Margot said, her mischievous eyes twinkling. "Hell hath no fury like a woman scorned."

***

Desmond sat on his couch as he watched the TV play news highlights the following evening. So far, Margot was doing well to keep herself quiet and make herself scarce. There were times it felt like he was living on his own, until he would see her come to the kitchen to collect some food and drink. She would not receive her first test on how quiet and scarce she could be until a time when Chantelle was to stay over again. She was supposed to have done so that night, but there was a change of plans.

"I have to go to dinner with my Mum tonight, sweetie. Perhaps we can reschedule for next week?" Chantelle had suggested over the phone, to his great relief.

His nerves could not handle the prospect of Chantelle finding out about Margot's stay. He already regretted agreeing to do this ridiculous favour for her.

As with so many other issues, Desmond chose to ignore it, filing it away to the side of his mind so he could focus the front on the task at hand. The task at the moment was absorbing the news he had missed over the past few weeks.

Another interesting news story about President Ezra Elbaz was playing. Desmond studied the still image of their national leader's smiley face. He looked young enough to have been his wholesome older brother, only a few years senior. A collection of newscasters stood in front of and around an edited-in graphic underneath his image, detailing all of the president's latest feats as they gushed over him. These were the highlights:

1. He recently participated in a charity marathon to raise money for underprivileged children in the capital city. Not only had his presence and participation alone allowed for them to vastly exceed the monetary goal, but he was a minute away from beating the marathon record.

2. He recently aided a group of scientists in making a discovery that helped make Slaek-metal more malleable. He did this by providing insights from pieces of independent research he had done on his own accord.

3. He held the highest approval rating for any world leader at the time. 80.4%.

At times, Desmond did not believe the man was real. Either his vast achievements were exaggerated by the media, or he was an alien from the Planet Zeus posing as an Earthling politician. He was too perfect, too beloved. It made Desmond simultaneously distrust and adore him.

Desmond found himself thinking about the president much more often. Ezra Elbaz's status was his ultimate goal and what he hoped to make of himself after climbing the ranks of RealSlack Research Firm.

To establish himself as a key figure and become even a fraction as successful and admired a person as he was. That was the dream.

SING, SCHEME

A SINGER. As Desmond stepped out of the car that dropped him back on his old neighbourhood street, he talked to Chantelle over the phone and learnt this was what she wanted to become before she joined RSRF.

"A singer?" Desmond asked, smirking as he walked away from his car and down Pennydill Road.

"Yeah," Chantelle chuckled. "Does that surprise you?"

"Not really. You have the classically beautiful look of a stage performer."

"You're such a flatterer."

"When did you quit singing? Before or after you got recruited?"

"Before, like a couple of years before. I realised my dreams of being paid to write music and sing were dead before RSRF was an option for me."

"Why? What happened?"

"Slaek happened, obviously."

"What's Slaek got to do with it?"

"Most entertainment media nowadays is mass produced by a few companies using the top Slaek Devices to operate and move large pieces of machinery to make works of art faster than dozens and dozens of humans ever could. The few performers that are still given a chance to make music have to *also* be experts in using Slaek on stage as well as dealing with the high probability of being replaced before their careers have even taken off," Chantelle detailed. "RSRF was, weirdly enough, the much more stable career choice for me when I was considering my future options."

"Makes sense," Desmond sighed with disappointment. With how much he was enjoying the perks of his job at RealSlaek, the hatred he used to have for Slaek's impact on the world at large had been tempered. The cognitive dissonance that came with working his new job was unbearable when faced. Hence why he chose to never face it, pretending it did not concern him in the slightest.

"There's a bright side to everything. If you had gone off to gallivant as a singer, you never would have realised the privilege of knowing me," Desmond quipped cockily.

Chantelle laughed. "Yes, that's right. I never would have met the great Desmond Eze," she giggled. "That would have been a very unfortunate fate."

The couple shared a heartwarming laugh. Dimples formed at the corner of Desmond's cheek as he let out a satisfied smile. "Alright, Chantelle, I'll talk to you later," he said, having finally walked to the middle of the street in front of his old home.

"See you, love," Chantelle signed off, blowing a kiss over the line before she hung up. As Desmond slid his phone back into his pocket, he opened the door to the home.

After two and a half months of gruesome RSRF missions, he was able to purchase it, meaning he now owned two homes. An impressive feat considering the state of the Renyland economy at the time. 80% of people in Desmond's generation would never be able to own even one. That, in a roundabout way, was what he found most impressive about President Ezra Elbaz. That the country he ran could be in such a dire state, yet his leadership was approved of by the vast majority of its people. Desmond was amused at how much the record-making charity runs, scientific discoveries, and cheerful smiles did wonders for the leader's image.

Despite having no practical use for it, Desmond saw it important that he purchase the house. Not only out of a nostalgic wish to own his childhood home, but to have somewhere to stay anytime he was hit with the urge to visit Ivrear without having to go back to Westout Street. He relaxed in his empty home during his day off, planning to do nothing but invite a friend over.

***

"Can't remember the last time I was here," Alistair commented, looking around the bare walls of the renovated living room. The only piece of furniture was four cushions Desmond laid out on the floor for them to hang out on. "I used to love coming to this part of town as a kid."

"The old Eze family home before we moved to the neighbourhood," Desmond reminisced as he too looked around. "I haven't seen these walls since 2012."

"Yeah," Alistair sighed as he leaned his head against the wall. He turned to Desmond. "I'm surprised you called me up, bro. Didn't think you'd have the time anymore."

"I've got to cut out time for you at some points. We haven't talked since after we escaped that block party," Desmond said.

"The block party," Alistair muttered. His neck lowered as if his head had grown heavy. He sighed softly out of his nose and clenched his jaw. Desmond had never seen his boisterous friend so low in energy. Now that it had come to mind, Desmond thought it was best to finally bring up the elephant dampening the atmosphere in the room. The massacre at the block party.

"How are you feeling about what happened that night?" Desmond asked. "Looks like it's still getting to you."

Alistair sighed. "I'll be fine. Not the first time I've seen people killed by cheap guns and cheaper Roef Devices," he chuckled awkwardly. "It is what it is. Shit like that is bound to go down in a neighbourhood like that every once in a while. Not like it's anyone's fault."

"Yeah, right," Desmond sighed, trying his hardest not to succumb to the mountain of guilt that was wearing him down.

He often thought back on the massacre he caused that day. Sometimes out of the same guilt that was eating away at him at that moment, most of the time out of a morbid fascination with it. The way those bullets curved through the air and multiple people's heads was quite the sight. It was the first time he had ever personally used a Slaek Device with such skilful potential about it.

"You've got a new job, haven't you? The one you mentioned on the phone? At the Slaek business?" Alistair asked. Desmond nodded. "What part of it did you say you worked in again?"

"The Market Research and Product Development Division," Desmond said.

That was what he and all the other members of their particular mission division were told to say when asked about their roles at RealSlaek RF.

Desmond imagined there would be hell to pay if he told his friend the truth. Such as the fates of the anti-Slaek-legislation lobbyists Chantelle had blackmailed the previous weekend. An interesting mission that he was jealous of.

"Ah, right, nice," Alistair said, somewhat impressed. "You get to work with a lot of Slaek, right?"

"Not a lot for my role. But when we do, we get to use top-of-the-line equipment," Desmond said.

Alistair nodded. "And you have access to Slaek lockups, where they keep this equipment?"

Desmond sat up with growing suspicion. "Why'd you ask?" he asked, not hiding the fact that he found Alistair's questions strange.

Alistair ceased with the hinting, speaking his thoughts clearly. "I'm thinking that your new job can be used as an opportunity for the neighbourhood. If you're *really* able to access a huge chunk of Slaek tech," he told Desmond.

He disliked the sound of this *opportunity* so far. "Do you want me to steal Slaek for you to sell on the streets, Alistair?"

"No wonder they hired you. You're as sharp as ever," Alistair laughed.

Desmond sighed with disappointment. "We were just talking about the shit that went down at the block party. How cheap Roef Devices caused all of that shit, curved all those bullets, killed all those people. Why would the neighbourhood need more devices like that around?" he said. For a second, he even believed the fake Roef story RSRF had passed on to the media as a cover for his mission.

"You said it yourself. *Cheap* Roef Devices. These will be high-level Slaek Devices pushed through the streets. You heard what they say on the news, we need more of those in neighbourhoods like ours! We're technologically underprivileged and shit!"

"Yeah," Desmond said, thinking back to those quotes from celebrities and politicians about increasing the number of Slaek Devices distributed to low-income areas. The same rhetoric that lined his pockets was now biting his backside.

"Come on, Des, just sneak out a couple for me to sell off. I could do with the money."

"Aren't there other ways you can make money on the streets? I think you going back to dealing drugs would *still* be less dangerous than what you're suggesting."

"Please, man, don't make me beg!" Alistair exclaimed. Desmond considered.

All of a sudden, he had an epiphany. In an instant, Desmond realised this situation could be used to his advantage. A dark plan brewing in the recesses of his mind was barrelling to the forefront. He took a deep breath out.

"I can't risk stealing them myself, I need this job. But I could pull some strings so that your boys could do it," Desmond explained. "I could arrange for some guards to be distracted and cameras to be taken down long enough for your guys to do a quick hit and run on a warehouse before the firm notices. There's a girl I knew at uni who works with me now. Margot. She could help me out with that."

Alistair's eyes lit. "Shit, you serious? You'd do that?!"

"I would. As long as neither you or anyone I know well does the job. Send some other guys you know in, and I'll make sure they can rush in and rush out with the stuff. I *won't* if you or anyone I'm able to recognise is there."

"Why can't I do the job? You know I like doing my own dirty work!" Alistair protested.

"I'm not arranging anything if you or anyone I know is planning on showing up for this heist," Desmond insisted. "I can't risk the small chance they connect the missing Slaek Devices back to me. If you can't accept that, then I can't accept this plan of yours."

Alistair grunted with frustration. "Alright, I'll cut in some lads I know from Defrohwe Street, get them to do the actual robbery. Would that be better?"

"Much better," Desmond asserted.

Alistair scoffed, shaking his head with a smile. Desmond conjured up a fake smile on his part. On the outside, it looked as if he was doing a dangerous favour for his good friend at the risk of his job. But on the inside, he was cooking something entirely different.

There was another reason as to why Desmond wanted neither Alistair nor any person he knew from the neighbourhood involved. This robbery was to be part of a grander scheme that would take Desmond many steps closer to his ultimate goal of Elbaz-level success.

OVERSEE, EXECUTE

DARKNESS. Desmond sat in the pitch-black space of his apartment's front room. Not the buzz of a fly or the air of his own breath could be heard, an intense silence encapsulating everything around him. He turned on his phone, shining the sole light in the room onto his stern face. He tapped an application that activated the monumental thin-screened television that covered the wall in front of him. Bright lights of a fluorescent hue attacked Desmond's eyes. He narrowed them as he watched every section of the screen.

The television was split into many different screens, tracking different camera feeds of different locations in and around the city, including a motorway, an abandoned safehouse, and an eerie warehouse facility. Desmond crossed his arms, leaning back in his chair with a deep sigh as he tried to maintain focus on each screen at once.

When the clock struck eleven, he was set on edge, sitting up as he checked the first live feed in the corner of the screen. He waited with anticipation as he glued his gaze to the motorway feed. Eventually, a red car with a black passenger door drove down the motorway. Desmond checked the time. Five and a half minutes past what he would have liked, but not enough time to derail the rest of the plan. He checked the second screen in the top middle section. The live feed was a touch blurry, but he could make out a general image of two dozen guards patrolling a large, chrome-metal facility sectioned off by barbed wire in the middle of nowhere. As if each of them were being slowly possessed, they would leave their post in pairs as time went by. By half past eleven, only seven of the twenty-four guards remained. Right on schedule. Desmond did a quick but thorough overview of the other screens. No movement had been made in and out of the safehouse from all directions, the live feed of an open field had been uninterrupted but for a rogue fox running across the screen, and the police station in the city centre was well lit.

By midnight, Desmond came to the satisfying conclusion that everything had either gone according to schedule or was just a few minutes behind or ahead of time. Nothing to worry about just yet. For the next twenty minutes or so, he could afford to not watch the screen so diligently and allow it to play in the background until he would need to act.

Desmond moved out of the imprint he made on his couch, walking over to lean on the island counter of his kitchen as he flicked through his phone. He relaxed for a moment and pulled up a pre-recorded video he had been meaning to watch the whole day.

His face flashed a duller screen blue from the fluorescent background of the cleared news station debate room, where a series of men argued around a table. These were clips from a debate that had been broadcast that morning, one he missed due to having to finish a RealSlaek mission. The debate, ironically enough, was titled the cheesy but apt *World War Slaek* by the TV presenters. It featured Thomas Lange, the Prime Minister of Vrelmany, a large, brutish, sharp-featured light-brunette man, arguing against Ezra Elbaz, President of

Renyland and a common fixture on Desmond's phone and mind as of late. They had been going back and forth recently on whether Elbaz's proposal for creating cities which ran on a shared "Slaek-Grid" would be a good idea. An idea he regularly brought up that would basically mean living in a small compacted community where no one had to use their own Slaek Devices because everything ran on Slaek installed in the very grounds and infrastructures of said community. Desmond was not sure whether he would want to live in such a place. Elbaz argued it would be a net positive for either country, and Lange could not disagree more.

"This idea for a Slaek-City you're proposing will undoubtedly go down in history as the greatest misappropriation of the tech of the 2020s. I trust when you say you believe it will 'build communities' you *think* you're telling the truth, but I and many others will tell you this vision of yours will only succeed in further atomising the people into secluded sections of the community you wish to foster," Thomas Lange argued passionately. "I'm all for visionary applications of emerging tech, but not at the expense of the people. Especially not my people."

Desmond knew what he was implicitly referring to. He had seen the statistics about young people in Vrelmany. Slaek Device usage *did* mean people left their homes less. Why go outside to engage with your community when you could have items ordered online and floated around your house with Slaek? Or why socialise at all? Once on a night out, Desmond had heard a few kids in their last year of high school talking about a masturbatory contraption they made so they would not have to worry about trying to have sex with actual women. From what Desmond understood, they would wear a headset and flash videos of a woman who spoke sweet nothings to them, then they would place one Slaek Device around their penis, pushing it down to the base and place another around the head. They said they would activate both so they would polarise each other and push and pull in a stimulating motion. He had seen multiple people talk about it online and even heard that one of Alistair's friends had tried it with Roef Devices, which did not end well. Desmond was almost certain these nasty Slaek Device-based sexual trends had started in Vrelmany of all places. He could understand Lange's worries about the community.

"Anyone who has done research as extensive as I have will tell you the exact opposite. In urban areas, 75% of citizens report feeling disconnected from their greater community, with 63% reporting they've never had the privilege of using Slaek Devices and 80% agreeing that being given the chance to would readily improve their lives," Ezra Elbaz retorted in equally passionate rebuttal. "Especially the 32% of both our nations that are elderly, not to mention the 23% who are disabled, as well as many others in a position that would be greatly improved by a connected Slaek-Grid taking the load off of their daily duties and easing their weekly woes."

That was one of Ezra Elbaz's primary skills. The man could list out dozens of statistics from memory faster than most could with a written list in front of them. The leader of his nation seemed to be winning the debate, much to the dismay of his brutish Vrelmany counterpart. Desmond leaned over, rubbing his chin, listening to the debates. He hung on Elbaz's every word.

"You're so obsessed with him," he heard the mocking voice of an irreverent female say.

Desmond's face soured as quickly as his mood as he turned to see Margot had slinked behind him. She leaned over the other end of the kitchen's island, her back arched and mischievous smirk squirming.

"You're still here?" Desmond scoffed.

Technically, the agreed-upon timeframe for his favour had passed. She was supposed to have packed her stuff and returned to her place by midnight. Margot pedantically reminded him she did not consider it a new day until she had slept and awakened. Among other excuses.

"Patience, Eze dear. They're still wrapping up the operations in my room and un-fucking the cameras," Margot said, trickling her fingers down his arm. "They'll be done by tomorrow, and I'll be back in my own place so quick you'll start to miss me."

"Can't wait," Desmond grunted, brushing her fingers off. He played another video on his phone, a continuation of the Slaek-City debate. Margot took this as an invitation to creep closer to him, making sure her hair dangled in the way of his screen as she rested on his shoulders.

"Do you mind?" he complained.

"Sorry, am I bothering you? Wouldn't want to interrupt your one-hundredth President Elbaz video marathon," she chuckled sarcastically, placing a smooth hand at the back of his neck. "Surprised I haven't caught you tugging one out."

"Mind your own business, I can watch what I please," Desmond scoffed, yanking his neck away from her.

Margot laughed. "Someone's even touchier today."

"Yes, so stop touching me."

"Don't you like it?"

"No."

Lies. A part of Desmond did like it, but he would never admit such a thing to her. He had to control himself in the face of Margot's incessant flirtations. From what he knew of her back at Hercole University, she only dated women but *fooled around* with men often. Even if he was not with Chantelle, he would not want to start fooling around with Margot. The woman seemed to be living, breathing trouble.

For the next few minutes, Desmond struggled to drone out Margot's pestering noise as he rewatched the sections of the clips she kept interrupting. He was about to replay the third clip a second time until he caught a glimpse of the time on the clock in the corner of his phone.

"Shit!" he exclaimed, rushing back to the couch.

"What's the matter with you?" Margot asked.

Desmond switched the multi-screen, swapping to close-camera footage of the dark insides of a facility storage room.

The first event he witnessed on the screen was a man's chest being blown open. One of the Defrohwe hoodlums Alistair had hired brought out a gun in self-defence. He paid the price for it. A group of agents in black leather jump suits, masks, and equipped with Slaek Devices, had cornered the Defrohwe gang, surrounding their red car with the black door. As soon as the unfortunate thief raised his gun, it was ripped out of his hands by the powerful magnetic force of Slaek and turned against him. A flick of a finger and the agent set off the trigger of the floating weapon, unloading rounds into the man's chest until a gaping hole had formed.

It took but a mere moment for the other thieves to panic and retreat. As they attempted to flee, the agents closed in on them. With synchronised twisting wrists, they increased the magnetic capabilities of each Slaek Device equipped on their person, tearing pieces of metal from the getaway car, and floating these pieces in tandem with their seized guns to close the hoodlums into a circular trap. Desmond leaned in as he watched the trap spring. If he had been distracted by Margot's antics for any longer, he might have missed the most important phase of his plan.

Desmond dove into action, too. He retrieved a Slaek Device from underneath a cushion and fastened it to his wrist. With a wave of a hand, he changed the close-camera feed to only show the live footage of the police station. He picked up his phone and rang the number "21213". The other line picked up. Two seconds of silence passed, then the other line hung up. Desmond put down his phone and watched the screen. The well-lit police station dimmed instantly, with all its lights being shut off one by one until it seemed as if the station was never open.

A minute later, a lone police car left the station. Desmond sighed with relief as he switched the close-camera feed back to the agents dispatching the thieves.

The floating circular trap of Slaek-controlled guns and metal turned into an autonomous firing squad of bullets and shrapnel that peppered and sliced through the Defrohwe thugs as if they were fine meat.

These thieves could have been killed in less cruel, simpler ways that would have sufficed, Desmond thought. One thug's nose was broken by the butt of a rifle, and as he reached a hand to cover his leaking face, his unprotected genitals were blasted to chunks by the same wavering weapon. Another thug had the barrel of a pistol thrust violently into his mouth, and the corners of his lips bled. Tears involuntarily poured out of his eyes before the inside of his head was reduced to a squishy pile of brain and bone over the warehouse floor. One particular man was given a uniquely cruel killing. An agent had equipped a minuscule pistol, throwing it in the air for the Slaek Devices to control. The magnetic force pulled at the trigger, controlling the bullet as it slit through one side of the man's neck, curved to pierce through another, then through one eye as he screamed in hapless agony, and then another, blinding him. The same tiny bullet made sure to curve itself and shoot through both his kneecaps, kidneys, and testicles multiple times over until he eventually died from a mixture of blood loss and shock.

Desmond could safely say he had never seen a man killed with such brutality before. His heart raced faster as each thief died. Another feeling he could safely say he had never experienced before was the delight brought upon by the death of others. Plan or no plan, it was atypical for him to be this excited after witnessing gruesome scenes.

"Easy now," he heard Margot chuckle in the background. He ignored her, watching the spectacle of dropping thugs until the warehouse had been well and truly cleaned of their presence. As the agents arranged the bodies, the quiet blaring of a single police car could be heard over the live video. The same police car that he had watched leave the station earlier.

Those quiet blares signified completion. The thieves Alistair hired had been executed, and subsequently, so had the main part of Desmond's scheme. Now all that he needed to happen was for the 'police' to do their 'jobs' and for the news story he drafted to be peddled through the right channels. Desmond smiled, his mind at ease.

"Fuck!" Desmond sighed, feeling as if his soul had been massaged and soothed. He reclined, sinking into the cushion as he muttered to himself with delirious delight. "It's done, man. All done."

"What was all that?" Margot asked excitedly, gesturing at the television Desmond was wiping the camera feeds from and shutting off.

Desmond laughed. He threw his phone and Slaek Device down and stretched his arms out behind his head. He was so satisfied with seeing the result of his machinations in real time that he did not care to reprimand Margot for cosying up to him on the couch. She draped one hand over his chest whilst the other travelled close to his crotch.

***

"What's the occasion?" Chantelle chuckled as she took two of the bottles out of his hands, placing them on the kitchen island next to her.

Desmond stormed over to her apartment the night following his successful mission, bursting the door down with three bottles of cognac and champagne in his hands.

"A job well done," he answered as he placed down the final bottle. He pounced upon her, ravaging her neck with his lips and tongue, grasping at her body like a beast.

Chantelle's excited giggles echoed through her apartment as she shut the door. Desmond was ready to give her the night of her life. She was ready to receive it.

***

Several hours of champagne-crazed sex later, Desmond sat on Chantelle's sofa in only his boxers. You could not paint a picture of a more content man, his cheerful whistles the only noise to be heard over the raindrop-esque patters from Chantelle showering in the bathroom.

Once again, Chantelle had helped him break his record for the best sex he had ever had. Multiple other recruits who lived close to Chantelle's apartment had messaged them complaining about the noise the day after.

That masturbation trend that people in Vrelmany and his neighbourhood had mentioned gave him ideas of how to boost the experience. With a dozen Slaek Devices placed all over the room and a dozen more worn around both of their arms and legs, Desmond and Chantelle had floating sex, soaring through the air as they ravaged each other's bodies. During said ravaging, he had held his load for a while, refusing to release until Chantelle had orgasmed multiple times. Once she had, he released, resulting in one and only one explosion that gave him the greatest euphoria of his life.

It was not just Chantelle's gorgeous, toned, voluptuous, brown-skinned body or the virile energy he felt that day that contributed to his euphoria. As he was thrusting inside her, he thought about the plan that caused this sporadic celebration in the first place. The power he felt from being able to succeed in a high-class mission of his own creation was a potent aphrodisiac.

During his orgasm, images of Defrohwe thug heads exploding from gunfire flashed through his mind, intensifying the pleasure of the experience. A highly concerning thing to have happened, but nevertheless, Desmond felt on top of the world.

And he could tell life was only about to get better.

CELEBRATE, PARENT

A GRAND CEREMONY. The second of which Desmond
had the honour of attending that year. Unlike his university
graduation, he enjoyed attending this one. No despondent,
gloomy glares this time around. He had only grateful smiles
for the RealSlaek employees who gathered in the
underground hall that day to celebrate their achievements.

He could not help but compare the two ceremonies
constantly. The RealSlaek fanfare in front of him effortlessly
blew last summer's Hercole graduation festivities out of the
water. Enormous chandeliers of maroon glass and the blood
red lights that hung from the ceiling could be interpreted as
giving the room an ominous tone, but it made everyone and
everything in it look vibrant, beautiful, and interesting. The
crowd seating area was a unique one, with the typical
efficient design of rows and rows of chairs in front of the
main stage being discarded in place for a complex star-shaped
seating arrangement.

Even the Slaek Devices attached around the hall at
Hercole had been upstaged at this event. Each side of this
blood-red room was decorated with maroon marble statues of
ancient and faceless mythological gods with Slaek Devices
placed around their ankles and wrists. It made it appear as if

their souls had been trapped within these fixtures and forced to do the attendees' bidding, floating around beverages and awards.

Throughout the ceremony, Desmond dissociated, just as he did during his university graduation. As opposed to the last time, where he did so out of depression, this time around, he did so out of excitement. He had been told ahead of time that he would be receiving a congratulatory ovation at the end of the ceremony. He could not think of anything else until then. All his attention went towards basking in glory in the very near future. He snapped out of this trance once he heard his name called on stage. By Sean MacGowan of all people.

"And now, let us band together and celebrate one of our exemplary new recruits, who showed what a RealSlaek employee can achieve with competence and initiative," Sean announced on stage. The only time Desmond had seen him express positive emotions that were not entirely faked or drenched in irony. "It's rare to see an employee with just a few months of experience work on organising and executing their very own mission from scratch and flawlessly succeed in the process. And yet Desmond Eze did exactly that with a few company resources and a lot of proactive will. This young man deserves a world of praise!"

"Yes, Desmond! Let's fucking go!" Jack screamed from the crowd, much to everyone's amusement. They joined in on his shouts and cheers of praise.

The fact that his mission succeeded so flawlessly still felt unreal to Desmond. The previous day, he saw that RealSlaek chose to go with the news story he drafted for the situation. What had been reported about the incident was that a group of desperate thugs tried to rob a Slaek Device facility and triggered the emergency alarm system. Police were called, the thugs opened fire, and the policemen, fearing for their lives, were forced to gun them down, believing them to be a greater threat than they were. No mention of how Desmond let these thugs into the facility, that no alarms were tripped, and that, aside from one police officer, no other patrol cars arrived at the scene until much later.

The police themselves corroborated the story and profusely apologised. All it took was some hefty bribes and an agreement to supply them with state-of-the-art Slaek tech. Both of which had to come out of Desmond's payroll, though he was more than willing to do this. The incident itself was framed as a sad tale of low-income young men desperate to take the tech that would help them and their community, and tragically losing their lives in the process. Slaek Device sales were through the roof at that point in time, the most profit the company had seen in months.

Desmond bowed, smiled, and waved at the rousing applause he received from the crowd. The section of other recently graduated employees roared the loudest. They were the most enthusiastic about his ascent in status. Bouquets of flowers and RealSlaek company care packages were floated onto the stage surrounding him to create a six-foot tower of rewards just above his head. His thanks of gratitude to the crowd could not be heard over their jubilation. He wished to live in this moment forever.

Shortly after, as Desmond stepped off the stage, Chantelle latched onto him before anyone else in the crowd could approach. She planted the wettest, most passionate kiss on his lips before pulling away. Desmond lovingly grasped her head and hair with both hands as he lost himself in her hazelnut-chocolate eyes. She leaned in close.

"Remember a while ago when I told you about the secret I had?" Chantelle whispered. "The one about my parents that makes other guys wary of me?"

"Yes…" Desmond muttered, eyebrows furrowed.

"I think it's time you find out all about it," she said. "But not from me. From them."

Chantelle had continued their relationship for quite a while without feeling the need to mention the secret until this point. Desmond held firm in his belief that it would be revealed on her terms, and now the day had come. He would have felt relieved to find out if it was not for how she said it. *Not from me, from them.* He had to prepare himself to meet *them*. The parents. The mysterious people who made the wonderful Chantelle Belle a romantic pariah.

***

Desmond followed Chantelle into a barren storage room, one of many strange, creepy, purposeless rooms that whoever designed The Hotel was very fond of. As he stepped in, the floors squeaked. He was hit with the sense that he was being lured to his death by his own girlfriend. As ridiculous and paranoid a thought as that was to have, Desmond clenched his fists, tensed his jaw, and narrowed his eyes in case he had to defend himself. He followed Chantelle as she turned a corner into an even emptier, eerier space of grey block stone. Waiting for them around the corner, standing completely still a few steps away, were the infamous Belle parents.

"Desmond, this is my mother and father. Mother and father, this is Desmond," Chantelle introduced.

Desmond kept a careful eye on both of these individuals. An unassuming couple on first observation. A frail, somewhat sickly, dark-skinned man and a plump, overweight, fair-skinned woman. The type of couple he would see trudging down a boardwalk whilst on holiday in Schvain. Their eyes, on the other hand, did not match the eyes of their innocuous holiday-faring physical archetypes. Both held a profound vacantness he only found in the most cruel and capable of individuals. Killer gazes, ones he had become accustomed to staring into whilst at RealSlaek. He figured out what the secret was along the lines of.

"Sir. Madam," Desmond said, greeting the pair of them.

"Nice to finally meet you, young man," Mrs Belle said, monotone.

"It goes without saying that Chantelle has spoken a lot about you," Mr Belle said, gravelly voiced. "Has it been the same the other way around?"

"Not really," Desmond said. Both Belle parents nodded in unison, satisfied with that answer.

"Would you like to find out more?" Mrs Belle asked. Desmond maintained enough control over his body to prevent an involuntary gulping of his throat. "I don't see why not," he said, masking his uneasiness.

Chantelle stood by as her parents closed the distance between them and a much tenser Desmond.

"We're very pleased with the work you were celebrated for earlier today. An employee as fresh as you are conducting a mission without being urged to by a higher-up, as well as using his own plans and money out of his own pocket to ensure it went smoothly, is an impressive feat. That's the type of work only expected of more seasoned employees at the very top," Mr Belle said. His killer gaze lasered in on Desmond in a manner he did not appreciate. He could hear his quiet grunting breaths as he did so. "You're aware of the type of people who become seasoned employees at the very top, aren't you?"

"No, but I'm assuming this is your way of telling me you're one of them?" Desmond guessed. The Belles gave him a confirming nod. Chantelle grasped Desmond's hand.

"My mother and father are some of RealSlaek RF's top employees. I'd actually go as far as saying they are amongst the highest-ranking employees currently alive," she revealed. She turned to the couple themselves. "Isn't that right?"

Desmond's head tilted down, anticipating the Belle parents' periodic physical tics, and matching them as the three of their heads nodded at the same time.

For once, he was not completely taken aback or even surprised by a revelation made at this firm. Of all the things he guessed beforehand about what the secret about her parents could have been, this was firmly in the top three.

"No offence, but is that all? Your parents are high-ranking RealSlaek employees?" Desmond scoffed. "This is why others avoid you? I don't get why this needed to be such a grand reveal."

"Of course," Chantelle muttered. Her eyes fixed on the floor as her parents took control of the conversation again.

"That's because you haven't truly grasped the situation that you're in," Mrs Belle chuckled without a smile.

"If there's more I need to know, then tell me, please," Desmond said with a sardonic flair.

Mr Belle broke away from his wife's side to get even closer to him. He placed a warm, constricting arm around his shoulder, leering over him as he held him in a comforting yet tight embrace. An unsettling intimidation tactic Desmond was familiar with being on both sides of.

"RealSlaek RF is like a family. Aside from being usefully blackmailed pawns with many fingers in many different pots, there's a reason the company hires so many employees.

Especially ones as young as you are," Mr Belle stated. "We're building a family to enter the new world with. It can't be done without the right type or number of people. Every faction needs its crop of elites. Understand?"

Desmond was not certain he understood, yet he nodded with the confidence of someone who did. Chantelle soon ironed out any wrinkles of confusion he might have had.

"You know the way most RealSlaek employees are held to their positions through pieces of blackmail the company holds over them?" Chantelle asked.

"I'm aware," Desmond sighed. Of course. Once a week, his mind flashed back to the infamous Sean MacGowan meeting at the seafood restaurant.

He had also learnt of Margot's blackmail story semi-recently. An incredibly ridiculous, elaborate story of how she accidentally cut off a Torteanese prince's thumb whilst out on holiday in Budai. The firm helped her cover it up during her recruitment process. A story he was surprised to find out was "not bullshit" as she showed him the proof. It was an even wilder blackmail story than Jack's beating of his baby cousin Harry.

"I'm one of the few cases in which that was not necessary. I'm the child of two of the highest-ranking RSRF officials. I've known company secrets since I was old enough to remember anything. I was born pre-blackmailed and can never leave RealSlaek, not even after my parents die. Mine and the company's fates are one and the same," Chantelle admitted, her voice hoarse and laced with concern. "Considering the direction our relationship is heading in, your fate will soon be the same. Understand?"

Desmond watched as all pairs of Belle eyes homed in on him. "Not completely," he admitted this time.

Mr Belle hugged him tighter. Mrs Belle closed in to rest a hand on his other shoulder. Chantelle held his right arm up with both her hands, placing it over her rapidly beating heart.

"Of all the potential suitors in the company, you are one of the only young males I've determined is deserving of my daughter," Mr Belle said.

"You'd have the most beautiful and intelligent children together, I can already tell," Mrs Belle added with a smile. "I'd be delighted to find out if you've already started the breeding process."

"That's…nice to hear," Desmond uttered with an awkward smile. That, for one, was not in the top thirty things he guessed he would hear during this reveal.

"Once we started getting serious, Desmond, you signed an emotional agreement. From now on, you are a part of a RealSlaek family," Chantelle said. "From now on, just as with everyone else in this room, your fate is tied to RealSlaek RF. You will be deeply involved in all of this for life."

Desmond could not decide where to focus his gaze. Everywhere he looked, hypnotising Belle eyes waited for him. A brief sense of dread washed over him as he contemplated what he had put himself into. For a second, he wished he had quit whilst he was ahead, taken the warnings of Jack and the other RealSlaek young men, and not involved himself with her. That brief moment of anguish and regret quickly passed as he thought more about his situation. He realised that in reality, it had barely changed.

"In order to successfully leave their job at RealSlaek, an employee would have to be fine with either having their dirty laundry list of company-held blackmail released to the public, or being murdered the second they officially cut ties. *All* RealSlaek employees are involved for life. Whether their involvement is shallow or deep," Desmond explained in response. "Right now, unless you can show me otherwise, I see that the only difference between me and most other employees is that I'll probably know more company secrets due to being deeper into *the family*. Either way, I'm still in this for life. It's the same path with extra steps."

"Secrets aren't the extra steps," Mr Belle chuckled. "These are."

Chantelle's father brought out his phone and swiped towards his RealSlaek RF schedule. He showed a series of codes in flashing red text that Desmond did not recognise.

"These are the missions I'll have to do now?" Desmond assumed. Mrs Belle confirmed with a closed-mouth chuckle.

"You'll be expected to *intern* on a lot of these upper-echelon and high-risk missions my parents conduct, such as I have in the past few months," Chantelle said.

"Upper-echelon and high-risk," Desmond repeated in a concerned mumble, the cryptic red codes sharp in his eyes.

"Any mission you've done so far does not compare to what you'll be helping us do very soon. Employees of your rank are used to doing one solid mission every once in a while, and getting to see the impact of your work discussed on the local news. Or, as part of some fleeting series of trending Slaek-stories that captures the nation for a week before being forgotten for the next," Mr Belle explained. "But have you ever been responsible for a phenomenon that occurs subtly over time through little increments until it eventually explodes into something of great magnitude? Exploding into a story or event that permanently changes the world? One that cements itself into the cultural and political zeitgeist of our era? That is the type of work *we* do."

Mr Belle's words were chilling enough to have Desmond adjust his back by straightening his spine. The scale at which higher employees operated was unforeseen during his time at RSRF thus far.

"52% of employees with that type of mission schedule die each year," Mrs Belle said.

"Jesus. Over half?" Desmond asked.

"Over half," Mr Belle confirmed.

"Most aren't capable of taking on harrowing levels of responsibility. Are you?" Mrs Belle asked.

The tinge of dread was returning, slowly circling through and tightening Desmond's chest like a choking black smoke. He remembered how wracked his nerves were whilst conducting his self-directed mission. And that was considering he was not even there in person to see and manage its execution hands-on. To have to experience that stress twice as much during missions where he would take a hands-on approach on a regular basis was unappealing.

Despite all of these feelings, Desmond shook his head as if the anxieties that were clogging it could be poured out of his ear like swimming pool water.

"I don't see the problem with having harrowing responsibilities. It's exactly what I need," Desmond said, his ultimate goal in mind. If he were to be even a fraction as successful as Elbaz was, interning during upper-echelon high-risk missions was the way forward.

"Really? You're okay with things being this way?" Chantelle asked, equally surprised and relieved. She gripped his hands in hers, tight enough to make both their palms red as she looked at him with doe eyes to die for.

Desmond chuckled. The more he thought about his goal, the more he became truly convinced he was actually in the *best* situation possible.

"I've always wanted to earn a raise in my company rank, and now it's being given to me by my wonderful woman and her devoted parents," Desmond said with a malevolent smirk. "If anything, I should be thanking you for this revelation."

FLY, DIE

THOMAS LANGE. He was the prime minister of Vrelmany, the country that could have been considered Renyland's greatest allies throughout most of this world's history. That started to change during the late 2010s and worsened during the early 2020s. Though their leaders were amicable with each other on the surface, there was clear tension between them.

The last time Desmond had seen Lange was during those news clips he watched where President Ezra Elbaz defeated him during the Slaek-City debate. That morning, Desmond saw Prime Minister Thomas Lange in the flesh with his own two eyes, standing a baker's dozen of people ahead of him in a queue at the airport.

Seeing the tall, broad world leader in person was *still* not the most interesting event that was to occur to him that day. Alongside him, carrying the lightest luggage one could, was the entire Belle family. Chantelle and her eerily calm parents.

Desmond and his girlfriend were to join her parents and help them conduct the first of those *upper-echelon high-risk missions*. He blamed his sweat on the humidity of a new country and the glaring lights reflected off the glass ceilings at the airport, but he could not even fool himself. Desmond was disquiet in comparison to the statue-like and empty forward stares of Mr and Mrs Belle on either side of him and Chantelle. He continuously stared further into the crowd at the back of Thomas Lange's head every other minute.

When the prime minister first arrived at the airport, hundreds of people attempted to swarm him, delaying the flight queue for an hour. Countless men with black suits and ear pieces hovered around the general queue, whom Desmond assumed were bodyguards preventing such a thing from happening any longer. It left Mr Lange able to scroll through his phone as he walked down the queue in peace.

The fact that he was able to see a world leader in real life for the first time was not what surprised him the most. It was the fact that said world leader was waiting in the same line as they were, planning on boarding an economy class plane, when a man of his status could afford a private jet. Come to think of it, they were four RealSlaek employees, and therefore *also* out of place. With two of them being top seniors at RSRF, they had purchased tickets for a plane that was fathoms below the high-class travel experience they were financially capable of obtaining.

Desmond understood the premise and goal of the mission at hand, but he would have liked to know much more. Chantelle's parents were adamant in their refusal to give him the reason for, purpose behind, or background of the mission.

Chantelle grabbed his attention with a tickling pinch to his sides. "Hey, don't stare so much!" she reprimanded with a chuckle. Even when telling him off, her voice was sweet to his ears. "Are you trying to blow all of our covers?"

"Thomas Lange," Desmond whispered, ignoring her reprimands as he stared even harder. "Why's Vrelmany's Prime Minister flying economy class?"

Chantelle shook her head at him, rolling her eyes before giving him an answer. "It's part of Mr Lange's *man of the people* routine. He prefers '*simple travel alongside honest working men*' in his words. He's been seen taking the public trains in Vrelmany quite often."

"I don't see the point in all of that," Desmond said.

"Neither do I. With the number of guards he brings on his travels, and how often he gets pampered during them, he might as well be flying in a huge private jet," Chantelle scoffed. "Catching the same flight as Prime Minister Lange is what Vrelmans consider to be the luckiest thing that can happen to a person. When he flies economy, the attendants treat everyone else on the plane *much* better. Passengers get high-class treatment for low-class prices."

Desmond sighed. "I doubt they'll consider themselves lucky today," he said, taking note of the subtle buzzing of excitement from the other members of the queue surrounding them. Not a single one was aware of the four RealSlaek RF employees who had infiltrated their fortunate flight.

"You're right, I don't think they will at all..." Chantelle agreed, her voice trailing off.

***

Much later, all passengers had boarded the plane and it had taken flight. Desmond sat in the middle of the plane's front section, occupying a seat next to an aisle with Chantelle sitting next to him on one side, and both her parents sat in the next aisle of seats across from them.

Desmond looked over to Thomas Lange. The prime minister occupied a seat at the front row of their section, far away enough to almost miss with a glance. Only the tufts of brunette hair from the Vrelmany leader's tall head could be seen from the angle in which they were seated. Desmond sat more comfortably in his chair, calming himself. As long as even a fraction of him was still in sight, all was going to plan.

At this point in their flight, he understood what Chantelle meant when she said Lange's presence changed an economy class flight. Most of the row of seats the world leader sat on, as well as half of the seats in the row behind him, were filled with his suited-up bodyguards. At the moment, Lange was being attended to by various members of the flight crew, especially the air hostesses who showered him with copious amounts of in-flight privileges, from massages to gourmet food. The hostesses who were not attending to him worked double-time in providing amenities to the rest of the grateful passengers on the flight. Desmond received a premium-quality neck warmer as well as the best coffee he had ever tasted during the first few hours of that flight. A far cry from the last time he flew with this company, AirVelrous, where his headrest was damp for no particular reason and the only drink they served was lukewarm sugarless tea.

"God bless Vrelmany," Desmond sarcastically quipped to Chantelle. She took a break from her coffee sipping to slap him on the shoulder as she laughed.

As Desmond scoped the scenario out, he noticed the profound lack of Slaek Devices present. Ever since the establishment of the Slaek Travel Act 2020 under Evincop Continental Law a couple of years ago, it was commonly understood that you could not even bring a Roef Device with you onto a plane for fear of its potential interference with the aircraft. But once the plane itself took off, flight attendants should be using Slaek equipment, especially air hostesses. He assumed the lack of Slaek on this flight was the crew's way of appeasing Thomas Lange's sensibilities. The prime minister had always been somewhat against how common

Slaek Device usage had become, but recently, he had taken up a position of active, intense dislike for the technology itself. He had not taken the result of his debate against President Elbaz very well.

Only one piece of Slaek had been brought onto this flight, though it was out of everyone's sight. Desmond knew where it was. He glanced over at Mr Belle. Chantelle's dad was in possession of a capsule from a miniature device, sneaking it on the flight by hiding it under his tongue.

Something less important caught Desmond's attention for a while after. He turned his phone back on, seeing a series of missed call notifications from hours prior, most from when he would have been at the airport. All from Alistair.

He stared at the red text that read "5 Missed calls from Alistair Armstrong", shaking his head at it. That had to be the tenth time Alistair had tried to contact him since the night the Defrohwe thugs he hired were killed at the Slaek facility. Which meant it was also the tenth time Desmond had intentionally missed his calls. He had half a mind to block his number, but he thought that would only make matters worse. He could already hear the rage-fuelled tirades Alistair would delve into were he ever to pick up one of these calls. Despite the rare paranoid thought, Desmond knew there was no way in hell Alistair would find out he had intentionally set up that whole warehouse massacre to the point of pre-writing the news story that followed it.

Still, Alistair had every reason to be furious after what had happened. From Alistair's perspective, Desmond had promised to be able to sneak the gang of thieves he paid into a Slaek Device facility, a task that not only miserably failed but ended in every single one of their deaths. For that reason, Desmond thought it best to wait a whole while longer before he as much as spoke to his childhood friend again. The thought of doing so alone gave him hypertension.

Desmond tried to force any thoughts about Alistair and his feelings out of his mind. He let out a deep sigh, adjusting his neck warmer as he sank into his seat.

"You alright?" Chantelle asked.

"Yeah, I'm fine," he said, resting his eyes half-shut. Chantelle rubbed a gentle finger against the side of his face, comforting him. "This mission will go down smoothly, don't you worry," she reassured him.

"It better," Desmond scoffed under his breath. He sent another studying glance to the back of Thomas Lange's head.

***

Hours later, Desmond had woken up from a slumber so deep he gasped for air as if he had been dead and reawakened. He felt majorly disoriented, both his vision and mind taking a while to unblur themselves as he blinked his eyes open. The skies outside the plane window had darkened, and the plane was much quieter, many passengers having fallen asleep for the night. What Desmond could last remember before his deep sleep was finishing the last of multiple glasses of complimentary champagne that the flight hostesses busted out. First for Lange, then for the others in their section.

"I don't think we should have any, considering what we're about to do," Desmond had advised.

"Let's have some, it'll be fine!" Chantelle had told him. Both of her parents gave the nodding go-ahead from across the row. They were permitted to drink their fill, and so they did exactly that earlier.

Now he had awoken from a disorienting slumber, not having the faintest clue of their mission status. He hoped to God that nothing had been compromised during his sleep.

Desmond's head darted in Chantelle's direction. "What's the situation?" he asked her.

Chantelle yawned. He found her sleepy eyes and the dopey smile that came with them to be incredibly endearing as she looked back at him. "We can chill now. Everyone's already finished up with their tasks."

"Everyone?" Desmond asked. He trusted all the Belles had done so, but he could not remember whether he had fully completed his assigned task.

"Those drinks really did a number on you, didn't they? You don't remember coming back from doing your task?" Chantelle asked.

Desmond thought for a second. Slowly but surely, it came back to him. His worries subsided as he realised that he definitely completed his task.

After he sunk his third glass of champagne earlier, he had walked passed Mr Belle's row of seats where he discreetly picked up the capsule from him with a sleight of hand grasp. During the commotion with the drinks being passed around the plane and passengers, he briefly snuck to the designated compartments near the crew rest areas where all the first aid kits and similar amenities were held. In quick time, he opened the capsule and used a piece of metal to pick out the Slaek residue. The oily material found at the heart of a Slaek capsule was advised to be kept away from most household items and appliances due to being both highly adhesive once out of its device capsule for a while, and prone to rusting and hardening once cooled.

With that substance slathered in thin but thoroughly applied lines across all the cabinet openings, and locks he could find, he had assured anyone who sought to open them would have to struggle for a while before they succeeded. He hoped no one was in dire need of a defibrillator or stitching supplies until the mission was complete.

"Yes, you're right, I did complete my task. It almost slipped my mind," Desmond said. "We're lucky I ended up getting it done. I knew I shouldn't have been drinking all of that champagne."

Chantelle chuckled as she rested her head against his shoulder. "All we have to do now is watch."

Desmond looked back in the direction of Prime Minister Thomas Lange. He tensed his jaw and braced himself for what he was about to witness. Ten minutes passed by, then fifteen, then twenty. Then, finally, as the young couple's eyes were glued to Lange's seating area, it happened.

"Fuck! Help!" the Vrelmany prime minister gargled.
He had unclipped his seat belt and leapt out of his seat, grasping at his throat. Blood pooled in his mouth and spurted out with every coarse cough and wheeze he made.

"Sir!" one of his bodyguards shouted in shock and horror, leaping out of his seat to help him.

The quiet, dozing rows of passengers woke up in collective horrified screams and shouts as the injured world leader ran around, spilling blood on the seats in front of and behind him. Their nice and calm day-long flight had turned into a frantic, petrifying, bloody mess of an evening.

The bodyguards attempted to take control of the situation, grabbing hold of the man who they were supposed to be protecting as he choked on fountains of blood. Such a hectic scene had been created around that section of the plane, such a wildly disturbed racket that the other row of bodyguards could barely contain it.

Desmond and Chantelle had to stand out of their seats to see all that was unfolding. Some of their fellow passengers and crewmates had rushed to his aid, grabbing hold of him as they desperately tried to figure out what was wrong.

A few of them joined the bodyguards in conducting full-plane searches of a first aid kit. They needed to find anything at all that could be used to help him. Thanks to Desmond's Slaek residue usage for lock and cabinet meddling, they could not reach a single useful appliance.

During all of this commotion, the flight crew finally sprang into action, offering their aid to the bodyguards and panicking crewmates who surrounded Lange. They had taken their time, returning to the scene with bottles of water, towels, and the only forms of antibiotics they could get their hands on without access to any of the medical cabinets. The pilot of the plane notified the passengers of the emergency landing they were soon to make and advised them to return to their seats. No one could hear him over the chorus of cries.

"It's strange what a mixture of gluten and peanut oil can do to an allergic man. When mixed with tiny shards of glass, I mean," Chantelle quipped, watching Thomas Lange drown in the thick crimson waves that poured out of him. She did so with as much interest as if it were an old show on TV.

Meanwhile, Desmond was more focused on how the flight attendants were dealing with aiding the dying man alongside the bodyguards and civilians. He had seen a few of the flight attendants act too roughly and sloppily with their handling of the prime minister. The grand show of incompetence displayed by the flight crew as they attempted to help the bodyguards halt the painful death of the prime minister was almost unbelievable to Desmond. He and the Belles were the only ones who knew this incompetence was intentional. They had been ordered to handle him in such a way as well as make use of the mixture that Chantelle had just mentioned.

She hid the glass granules and anti-Lange allergens in small bags through an orifice best not spoken about out loud in order to sneak them through the airport. Then, much earlier in the flight, she had moved as if she was to go to the bathroom, only to slip herself into the plane's kitchen to plant them there. The flight assistants had been helping them carry out the mission, putting subtle drops of tasteless peanut oil and sprinkling glass spread out into Thomas Lange's food and drink during every on-flight meal that was delivered to him. Hours and hours of meals and drinks later, the gradual allergic reaction plus internal haemorrhaging combination had finally resulted in this glorious display of spraying blood.

Mr and Mrs Belle had deployed the simplest negotiation tactics available to make the flight crew fall in line with their plans. Heavy threats and heavier bribes.

It seemed the blood that was to escape Lange's body was endless, pouring and pouring as he whimpered and twitched. The intentionally hapless flight attendants, plus nurses and the clueless bodyguards and civilians, were unsure of what to do as they wiped away the blood and made efforts to feed him water and antibiotics. Desmond shook his head at their poor efforts, faked or otherwise.

"Don't worry about whether the flight crew will snitch about their involvement in all of this. That's mum and dad's next mission," Chantelle whispered into his ear.

"They'll be killed even though they took our bribes?" Desmond asked, whispering back.

"Not quite. They'll be framed as having been the ones who came up with the plot to poison the prime minister. They'll have no proof to defend themselves against it, forced to stew in the global shame and punishment of it all for a little while," she explained plainly. "*Then*, they'll be killed."

If Desmond was not mistaken, he could hear a quiet giggle coming from Chantelle as she disclosed this to him. She tried not to make it obvious, but he could tell that thinking of the flight crew's fates delighted her.

Thomas Lange's blood-soaked struggles came to an end. There was only so much blood a person could cough as their throat tightened, and Lange had passed that limit. The plane descended into morose wails of further sorrow as his body stiffened. Vrelmany was to mourn their lost leader.

Desmond took a deep gasp out, not realising until that very moment that he had been holding his breath the entire time. He had never witnessed such a tense and gripping death. He did not even feel this shaken up the time he murdered the thug in the alleyway. The only time when he was this shaken up was when he had accidentally killed his siblings.

Desmond was surprised at how nonchalantly Chantelle treated the assassination. This was a unique experience for him, one he would never forget. He had played a hand in the death of one of the most powerful men in the world and was able to watch the life drain from his body in real time.

An amazing scene.

NETWORK, MURDER

A COUNTRY IN MOURNING. That was the phrase used to describe the state of Vrelmany. A month had passed, and another temporary leader filled Lange's former position, the country balancing itself on shaky ground. An 'investigation' was held in which it was determined that the assassination was conducted as a coordinated conspiracy by political rivals carried out by the plane crew. Every single pilot, flight attendant, and hostess had been accused of organising to poison him together. Most of whom were soon to be sentenced to life imprisonment, some of whom had supposedly killed themselves or been killed by disgruntled Vrelmans looking for vengeance for their fallen leader. This told Desmond that Mr and Mrs Belle had completed their mission just as Chantelle promised.

Those in heavy support of Slaek made not-so-subtle suggestions about how the prime minister's death could have been avoided had Slaek Devices been allowed onto the plane. The use of them could have halved the work of those who made efforts to help the suffering world leader and potentially saved him before it was too late, they said. Thomas Lange's legacy outside of Vrelmany was becoming that of a man whose hatred for technology contributed to a death that could have been avoided. Another portion of potent pro-Slaek propaganda at Thomas' expense.

On the other hand, his rival, President Elbaz, was thriving, being in the news again for his charity work. He was in the country of South Jabriga, where his team were helping poor Slaek miners with their workload. More favourable lights shone on the Renyland leader as their former national allies of Vrelmany continued to plunge into darkness.

Every once in a while, life felt surreal to Desmond. He had played a direct hand in this darkness and seen all rewards and no consequences. He could not make sense of it. Almost half a year working for RSRF and he was richer than most men his age could dream of being. Many more upper-echelon high-risk missions revealed themselves on his RealSlaek schedule, and the boldening young man was more than ready to complete each and every one of them.

***

Desmond attended yet another black-tie event held for the sole purpose of having the rich and powerful aimlessly schmooze with each other as they gave one another empty congratulations about whatever 'charity' or 'research' they were funding for the aid of a third-world nation. He had been to so many since he started doing higher-level work at RSRF that they all blended together.

None of the grand sights to be found there were as interesting to him as they were the first time he had seen them. Not the celebrities and politicians who he would usually only see on the news. Not the luxury blue carpets that felt as if your dress shoes were sinking into watery clouds. Not the complex light shows and the sleekest fixtures of Slaek Device turrets sporadically decorated in any spare space. Not even the giant cheque of an obscene figure with

103

far too many zeroes that had been floated around at the start of the event with fanfare. To think all of that money was raised and its only purpose was to be given away. A travesty, Desmond thought.

He could not enjoy anything at the event. He could only think of the mission he was to do by the end of it. A straightforward but potentially very stressful one. The objective of the mission would have made it so on its own, though the main source of Desmond's stress was the fact that Margot had been assigned as one of his two partners on it.

"Don't feel like networking anymore?" Margot joked. An intricately designed glass of a golden cocktail was floated into her empty hand as she approached him again. "Hmm?"

She sipped the cocktail and looked at him as if waiting for an earnest answer.

Desmond scoffed. "I wonder. Is there anything in your life you take seriously?" he asked, a smirk on his face in spite of the irritation her being around him caused.

"I take you seriously, you're a *very* serious boy," Margot chuckled. "You don't know how grateful I was when I found out I'd be on this mission with you. You've risen through the ranks so quickly, it's like I'm on a date with a top company official right now."

"Yeah, alright," Desmond scoffed. Before they had arrived at this mission, the two of them had rarely been in each other's presence at RealSlaek. The last time they had an in-person conversation was during the period she cashed in her favour and stayed at his apartment whilst hers was used for her temporary narcotics operation. He found he strangely missed the regularity of her bothersome quirks and semi-ironic flirtatiousness.

"You and Chantelle Belle seem to have a happy relationship," Margot commented.

"Thanks for noticing," Desmond scoffed.

"It's probably going so well because she hasn't found out about the time you let another woman live in your home and touch you whenever she wanted," Margot chuckled.

She brushed her hand against Desmond's chest. The same way she had done those nights they spent alone. Nights spent on his sofa, sitting in front of the screen as he planned his Alistair-hired-thugs massacre mission.

"Would it be fine if I broke that news to her? I'd really like to," she added.

Desmond scowled. "That better be a fucking joke," he grunted, glowering into the general crowd of black-tie attendees as he shifted to one side of her.

Margot laughed, her eyes following his every movement. "And what if it wasn't a joke?"

Desmond turned slowly, his eyes meeting Margot's. He stared with a quiet rage into Margot's dancing pupils. He held his scowl as he rested a hand on Margot's shoulder.

"You said it yourself. I've risen up the ranks fast, I'm like a top official now," he told her, his voice threatening as he gripped her shoulder. "Are you willing to find out what happens if you wrong someone in my position?"

Desmond stared down at her with daggers, tightening his grip with clenched and trembling fingers. Margot attempted to laugh the threat off and brush away his hand. She could not do either without having to exert more effort. He refused to let go of or break eye contact with her.

As he stared down at her, Desmond watched her mask of irreverence crack. The smug smile had been wiped off her face, replaced by a transient countenance of subdued fear.

Before Desmond could enjoy it for too long, it had faded with the return of her usual irreverence.

"Alright, Des, I'll leave you two alone," she chuckled in an effort to stop her body from shaking and regain her poise.

"Fantastic," Desmond scoffed as he slipped his hand off of her shoulder. He watched with gratification as she rubbed away the mark his heavy grasp had left there, almost as red as the dress she wore.

"What are you two doing?" a deep, coarse male voice asked with such gravitas that it compelled both of them to focus on him immediately. Perhaps they feared either of their covers had been blown. But it was far from the case.

The third member of this RSRF mission had returned. A tall, buoyant-haired recruit of the same age group as Desmond and Margot, with slim and icy sharp eyes that complemented the perpetual vexation he wore on his face. Of all the faces he had come in contact with at RealSlaek, this man possessed the most unnerving one, the clear contempt it held for Desmond whenever he saw it not helping.

"Hello, Lloyd," Margot said, smiling and waving with a twiddle of her fingers.

"I asked you guys a question," Lloyd grunted.

"Nothing, Lloyd, we're doing nothing at all. Go check the perimeter again," Desmond dismissed.

Lloyd scoffed, dismissing him in return with a wave of his hand without looking in his direction. The gruff RSRF employee mellowed out as he directed himself to Margot. He held her gently, placing one hand on the spot of her shoulder that Desmond threatened to tear off before he had arrived.

"You alright, Margot?" he asked.

"Yes, Lloyd. You mustn't worry about me so much," Margot laughed, holding his hand by the wrist.

"Mhm," he sighed. He gave Margot an awkward, endearing smile before giving Desmond the complete opposite expression. Desmond scoffed at him.

In the few days they had known each other, all Desmond was sure of was that Lloyd Gould did not trust him. This shoulder situation gave him more reasons, though Lloyd also struck him as the type to make a habit of mistrusting everyone regardless of their actions.

"What's the status of the target, Eze?" Lloyd asked, suppressing his frustration with Desmond to allow for mission professionalism.

"Mr Washington's still on the move but starting to slow down. The drink's getting to him," Desmond said, looking at the man mentioned through the corner of his eye.

"That hippie environmentalist cunt doesn't know what he's in for," Lloyd said, doing the same.

A boisterous man in a dark purple suit could be seen charming his fellow guests next to a white table at the right-centre section of the room. Whatever he was saying was incomprehensible to them, it only being obvious that the story entertained the guests, who were amused by his gyrating hand symbols that added flavour. He was their target for the night. Tyler Joseph Washington, a young up-and-coming politician from the United Regions of Zereneva known for his Elbaz-esque fast-talking eccentricities on one hand and, on the other hand, his un-Elbaz-like penchant for speaking out against the harm Slaek mining did to the environment.

The trio watched Washington as a Slaek Device floated a drink into his hand to replace the one he had finished. The Zerenevan raised an eyebrow at his refilled hand.

"I'll admit that these pesky machines are very convenient! It's a shame the disruption of ecosystems their manufacturing causes isn't!" Tyler Washington snarked, loud enough for a great portion of the hall to hear. "Oh well, maybe one day we'll learn our lesson. Maybe before the world burns? Fingers crossed!"

The crowds of people at the event smoothly erupted into affluent laughter at the young politician's snarky warning. Lloyd gritted his teeth at their reactions.

"You've dealt with the cameras, haven't you, dear?" Margot asked. Lloyd grunted a yes.

"Desmond, have you set up the timed call?" Lloyd asked.

"Yes. The call is being made as we speak," Desmond confirmed. In approximately twenty minutes, the guards who speckled the event would be too busy to deal with a potential bomb threat to see what the trio were up to. "Margot, how well would you say you've acquainted yourself with Washington throughout the evening?"

"Enough to lure him away when need be," she answered with a smile. Every once in a while, she had approached him whilst pretending to be an adoring fan, sharing a drink with him and then listening to his rambles for a few minutes before regrouping with either Lloyd or Desmond.

"As soon as he's away from that stupid crowd, move in on him again, Margot. And Desmond, as soon as she does that, you should time another call," Lloyd ordered.

Desmond disliked taking orders from him. Especially considering that he had been on twice as many missions of this calibre as either Lloyd or Margot, courtesy of his closeness with the Belle family. Despite that, he trusted his sour-faced mission partner's judgement.

"Alright," Desmond accepted with a nod. The trio dispersed.

***

Twenty-five minutes later, the hundreds of event attendees hastily crowded all entrance and exit doors in the area, ignoring the security guards' measured advice to evacuate the premises in single-file lines.

"There's a bomb? Is that what they said? Did I hear that right?!" one of the alarmed attendees asked the people around him in the crowd, breaking down the already weakening constitutions of his fellow event members.

Both of Desmond's encrypted calls succeeded in establishing mania.

As Desmond struggled to keep himself upright and untrampled through the fearful black-tie masses, he searched for his mission partners. Lloyd was at the front of the crowd, their portion of desperate attendees escaping through the north-west hall exit. Margot was harder to find. He perused through every cluster of attendees in every area of the hall to realise she was nowhere to be found. As was one of the most important attendees of the night.

"Has anyone got eyes on Mr Washington?!" one of the security guards desperately asked another. They had been asking each other some form of that same question for the past few minutes.

That meant that their misdirection succeeded, and Margot had escaped with the young environmentalist. Now he had to leave the event inconspicuously, evacuating from a different point at which Lloyd was and regroup with them after another lapse of time.

***

After waiting a while, Desmond reconnected with Lloyd. The two of them walked together through a street with enough dirt, grime, and trash cluttering it to rival a scrap heap.

They entered a wooden house that, from its poor condition, could be assessed to have been long abandoned. Parts of the doors and staircase railings fell apart when handled or slightly touched, and an ungodly stench carried throughout the abode, one that told Desmond that multiple people must have died there recently.

"Fucking shithole," Lloyd grunted in irritation as he and Desmond headed up the stairs and into the first bedroom. The two mission partners saw the third once they entered.

"Nice to see you again, guys," Margot chuckled. With a Slaek Device on her left wrist, she floated down a large briefcase from on top of a degrading wardrobe in the corner of the room. In front of her and the briefcase was Tyler Joseph Washington.

The young politician whimpered, a blindfold around his eyes as he struggled with the impossibility of escaping from the chair he was bound to. Slaek Devices were fastened around the wrists of his hands and feet, whilst also being attached to another layer of Slaek Devices attached to the chair itself. The magnetism from all these devices combined to ensnare him for however long Margot desired.

This was exactly how Desmond expected to see the unfortunate environmentalist once he realised Margot had already captured him and escaped. He did not expect Mr Washington to have been stripped naked.

"Who are you people?! Why are you doing this to me?!" Washington cried out. Tears poured out from beneath his blindfold, his thick curly hair flopping about as he attempted to wriggle free.

"Quiet, please, Tyler. You're making this worse for yourself," Margot chuckled. She planted a kiss on his lips, causing him to shut his mouth and freeze in shivering terror.

Desmond sighed at the sad sight. Lloyd, however, was enjoying it just as much as Margot was.

"Take a look at Mr Fast-Talking Enviro-Prick. All of a sudden, he's got nothing to say whatsoever," Lloyd mocked. "Shouldn't you be rambling about how Slaek Devices being built contributes to the devastation of climate change?!"

Washington's lips trembled. Desmond could practically hear his inner contemplations. Should he keep quiet like Margot ordered, or latch onto what Lloyd said and use it as a way to potentially escape? He chose the latter.

"Is that why you're doing this?! Did one of my rivals hire you?!" Washington asked.

"I thought I told you to be quiet, Ty," Margot chuckled. She reached a hand out and grabbed his penis, twisting its head between her thumb and index finger. After he finished twitching and yelping in pain, Margot let go of his member. Washington continued his attempt to talk his way out.

"I don't even believe in that eco-system destroying, climate-change-concerned, anti-Slaek propaganda bullshit! It's just rhetoric I parrot for votes!" Washington cried out. "If you let me go, you won't hear another word of it, I swear! I'll stop doing public talks in Renyland! I'll scrap my future plans for Zerenevan presidency! I'll expose my own scandals and tank my entire fucking political career!"

Desmond sighed again. Lloyd gritted his teeth. "All of what you're saying is having the exact opposite effect on me," he scoffed. "If anything, my desire to kill you has just soared through this shitty wooden roof."

Margot chortled. She clapped in appreciation of the same hostility in Lloyd that Desmond was not fond of. Washington became more distraught and aware of how hopeless he was, sweating and panting as every inch of him shook.

"Please! Please! Hear me out! Fucking please!" Washington begged through tears of blood. "All the money! I'll give you all the money in the world! You'll get way more than you'd ever be able to spend in a dozen lifetimes if you just let me go! Please!"

"Sorry, Mr Washington. We can't do that," Desmond sighed. The young politician burst into incomprehensible, snot-filled sobs. It was time for his execution.

Margot opened the suitcase she had floated in front of them earlier. Inside its velvet red interior were up to twenty-five different blades, all polished to perfection. The exact type of possession he would expect an employee like Margot to bring with her.

"Weren't we supposed to kill him discreetly?" Desmond asked, eyeing the daggers and knives.

"So?"

"How is cutting the shit out of him discreet?"

"They said we can kill him however we see fit, *D*."

"With the caveat that the way we see fit is discreet, *M*!"

"I don't care about the rules! I want to cut him to bits!"

"I don't care about what you want, I'm not letting you fuck up this goddamn mission!"

Lloyd placed himself between the arguing duo, glaring at Desmond as he protected Margot.

"Let the lady play as she pleases," Lloyd demanded.

Desmond grunted. He wanted to challenge him, but was keeping track of the time. If they spent any longer arguing about this, they would risk being caught wandering around this area, blowing their cover, and sullying the mission. He knew neither of them would give in, so he thought it best to allow them to *play as they pleased.*

"Fucking amateurs," he complained under his breath as he stepped away from both of them.

Margot giggled with satisfaction. She took a step away from him and towards Lloyd. She pulled the icy-eyed employee towards her, engaging in a spontaneous, sloppy tongue-kiss with him to show her gratitude. An act that surprised both Desmond and Lloyd himself.

"Would you like the first cut, sweetie?" Margot asked Lloyd as she released him. Lloyd wiped his lips, a malevolent grin about him.

"Definitely," he grunted with lustful excitement. In one singular movement, he grabbed a butcher knife from the suitcase and slashed Washington across the face.

The politician wailed, the bleeding gash on his cheek leaking into his mouth.

"I said shut the fuck up!" Margot screamed.
She picked out a thin knife from the suitcase and used it to slice a small wound across his urethral meatus. When he inevitably roared with unfathomable pain, she gave him a matching cut on his face and moved aside for Lloyd to take another slice at him.

Desmond watched her and Lloyd establish a back-and-forth cutting routine on Washington. Had the area they took him to not been completely abandoned, his screams would have been heard by the entire neighbourhood.

The last time Desmond had heard screams like that was during the final days of his brother's painful illness and subsequent death. Those memories made the execution just the more unbearable to watch.

Lloyd and Margot sliced and slashed at Washington's body. With each cut from one, the other would deliver another cut twice as swift and carving, as they competed to see which one of their blades would finish the job.

Neither of them won this competition. A bullet fired past the two of them and lodged itself in Washington's skull. A clean, bloody hole above his blindfold and below his hairline. Desmond had delivered the official killing blow. He sighed and returned the gun to the inside of his blazer.

"Let's finish here before anyone sees this," he ordered.

"You're no fun. No fucking fun at all," Margot groaned.

"Boring prick," Lloyd insulted in agreement with her.

Desmond ignored them both. He pulled out his Slaek tablet and searched his classified document notes for a reminder of RSRF's typical body-disposal procedure for high-status victims. He shook his head at the butchered corpse in the chair in front of him. Their next task was to blame this on thugs in the area, creating a scene to make it seem as if Tyler Washington had been involved in an unfortunate gambling incident with organised criminals.

Despite any faults he had, Desmond felt sorry for Tyler Washington. He was a bright up-and-comer with there being many similarities between him and a younger Ezra Elbaz in the late 2010s, before he had been elected as the president of Renyland. Unlike Elbaz had in the late 2010s, Washington would never rise to the position of President of the URZ. His story ended there, unceremoniously murdered in a rotting old house by Lloyd Gould, Margot Forster, and Desmond Eze.

The trio snuffed out that bright light, for the sake of lining their pockets and increasing the power of RealSlaek RF.

CUDDLE, LEARN

AWKWARD. Desmond had just returned from the most uncomfortable post-mission travel of his life. He had to assume those who organised and arranged the missions were toying with him. Amongst the seven people who had been assigned to Desmond's last mission were Chantelle Belle, Margot Forster, and Lloyd Gould.

Desmond led this acquainted group of RealSlaek employees. They were tasked with *Slaek Device Redistribution*. A series of missions where they would break into and steal Slaek Devices from the homes of middle-class owners and distribute these devices into poorer neighbourhoods, dumping them on the streets. Naturally, Desmond had asked why they were redistributing from the middle class to the poor and not stealing from the upper class and beyond. It could not be an issue with access, since he had killed multiple top-level targets by that point in his career, therefore, stealing major Slaek equipment from the same class of people would not be difficult. He received no answers from his mission-handlers other than irritated commands to "Just do your damn job."

Aside from the strangeness of it all, Desmond found it a relatively straightforward mission that was completed without as much as a minor hiccup. It was the mission return that was much more difficult to live through. As with the mission, Desmond was accompanied by Chantelle, Margot, and Lloyd. Unlike the mission, he was forced to occupy the same space for hours at a time, sitting amongst them in the back of the RSRF van as they travelled back to base.

Desmond warned Margot not to act up in Chantelle's presence, though it was clear such warnings had fallen on selectively deaf ears. Margot decided she was in the mood for more childish flirtations, engaging in a game of footsie with Desmond, to which he abruptly stopped with a shift of his foot. Not abrupt enough, evident by Chantelle's curious glance at both of them. Desmond's eyes shot quick daggers in Margot's direction. His cautionary scowl only proved to amuse Forster and inspire her to provoke him in any way that came to mind during their travels.

Every once in a while, she would touch Lloyd sensually, whilst glancing at Desmond midway through the act. Lloyd, of course, had no problem with this and would even grin like a madman during it all, encouraging her to continue. At one point, they kissed, with Margot making sure to look at Desmond out of the corner of her eye as she did so.

Once these antics ceased to have the desired effect, Margot moved on to touching Desmond himself, using every bump they met on the road to 'accidentally' fall forward into his lap up to four times.

"Oh shit, sorry," she would chuckle each time.

It was clear no one in the van thought it was accidental. Lloyd found it all especially hilarious. Desmond could feel a subtle rage radiating off of his girlfriend and the barely hidden disdain on her face throughout the whole journey. There had been many gruesome missions Desmond had participated in, yet that was the most agonised he had felt in a while.

***

Chantelle came to spend time with Desmond in his apartment later that day. She entered his home in a foul mood due to Margot's foolery, though she made no comments about it initially. It was forgotten, and her mood lightened. On the surface, at least. Desmond hoped that once they had all returned to The Hotel and separated as a group, that would be the last he would hear of it. A few hours into their day together, he thought that perhaps that was to be the case. As he relaxed with Chantelle on his sofa, he realised it was not.

"What's going on with you and that Margot girl?" Chantelle asked him ten minutes into the black-and-white movie they had been sitting and watching in silence. She tried to make it seem as if the question had randomly come to mind, though it was obvious to Desmond that it had been occupying her thoughts for the entire day.

"We went to the same university, Hercole," Desmond answered. "We've been assigned to quite a few of the same missions recently, too."

"Why was she doing all those odd things with that Lloyd guy and looking at you all the time?"

"She likes to make people feel uncomfortable, especially her so-called friends. It's funny to her, apparently."

"Hmm, she's very strange."

"She's stranger than you think," Desmond chuckled. Chantelle's soft face twisted into a hard grimace as she sat up. "What do you mean by that?!"

Desmond's eyebrows furrowed. He sensed he might have said something gravely wrong. He witnessed an unfamiliar wrath about her that was soon to surface if he misspoke.

117

"From the other missions I've been on with her, she's psychotic even for RSRF standards," Desmond said. "She completely ignored employee protocol on a mission we completed, simply because she thought it would be fun to *decorate* the target's skin with cuts of a butcher knife before killing him. She's strange *and* sadistic."

"Yeah, she is," Chantelle said. "I think both of us should try to avoid her from now on."

Desmond nodded in agreement. "The less I see of her in the future, the happier I'll be."

Chantelle calmed down, cuddling up to Desmond again with a pleased sigh. Their attention refocused on the black-and-white movie. Unfortunately for Desmond, only a few minutes passed before Chantelle decided to hit him with another round of questions.

"There's something else I've been meaning to ask you all day," Chantelle admitted.

"What is it?" Desmond asked, masking his exasperation.

"How come you've never told me about the blackmail RealSlaek threatened you with to bring you on to the company?" she asked. "I showed you mine. Introduced you to my parents and all."

"Does that really count? You promised to say the thing about your parents beforehand. It was the condition for this entire relationship," Desmond said, smiling.

"Come on, please tell! Don't you trust me?"

Desmond's face lit up with realisation. "Hold on, didn't I already tell you? On the way back from our holiday to Côte d'Magnifique?"

Chantelle thought. Soon her face lit up with realisation. "Right, the man you killed after he tried to rob you?"

He had blurted it out to her in an inebriated revelation on the flight home. That was another instance in which they had been unreasonably drunk together on a plane.

"See? I *did* already tell you."

"Alright, but what about the other piece of blackmail?"

"What other piece?"

"The one to do with your late siblings."

Desmond paused. He sat up, removing himself from her cuddling embrace. "How do you know about that?"

Chantelle's face darkened as she shifted from side to side.

"You talk in your sleep sometimes," she reluctantly answered. "Once you said something about your siblings being used as blackmail, too. I've seen you weep whilst you sleep some other nights. I'm assuming it's very painful for you to relive those memories."

Desmond's heart froze for a moment. All confidence and energy seeped out of him as he stared into space, gormless. His thoughts were blank, and his expression blanker. His sharp, dark brown eyes had widened until they appeared round and lifeless. His jaw clenched hard enough to shatter his ramus as he emitted a low grunt from his fastened mouth.

His reaction riddled Chantelle with distress. "I'm sorry, I didn't mean to upset you," she apologised, rubbing his chest.

"You didn't," Desmond asserted, lying.

"Why don't we talk about something else? Like our next holiday?" Chantelle insisted. "How does a six-star Budai resort sound? Or maybe the Altredene Alps?"

Desmond shook his head. "No, it's fine, I'll tell you about my siblings," he sighed. "Might as well."

"Alright," Chantelle said quietly.

She sat up straight, then leaned over him, desperate to hear all about it. Desmond lowered his head and cleared his throat.

"You know that disease from a few years ago that made the inside of your throat hard as rock and urine bloody? Pasbrut. You'll remember hearing a lot about it in the news back then," Desmond started.

"I do," Chantelle said pensively. "Didn't the government suggest that people shouldn't travel to certain countries until regular recoveries had been recorded in each?"

"Yes. There was a short period of time in which certain places still had their borders open, but you were advised to stay away. Unfortunately, as a reckless teen, I didn't care to listen. Me and some mates from school weren't very rich, so a holiday was a once-in-a-lifetime thing for us back in those days. At the time, Rosie, Ella, Alistair, and I had plans to travel to one of the countries on that list, and we weren't going to cancel them, Pasbrut or not," Desmond explained. "We spent a week in Dhanz, ending up having to leave earlier than we wanted due to the rising number of national cases. If we hadn't, we would have been quarantined with everyone else there the following week. We would have been trapped in a highly infected country for months."

"Oh my," Chantelle sighed.

"I thought as long as I kept myself safe, and my friends and I didn't go to certain areas, that I wouldn't even have to think about Pasbrut," he said. "I was wrong. Very wrong."

"Did you catch it?!" Chantelle gasped. "That must have been agonising to go through!"

"I did catch it. But my specific symptoms were completely undetectable. All I had was a rough cough and a dull pain in my bladder that went away after a week or so. I had no idea I was infected, and neither did anyone else," Desmond said. "I was allowed to come back into Renyland

120

and back into my family's home. Without anyone having a single clue about what I had. Including me."

Chantelle's eyes quivered with sorrow. "I see where this is going," she sighed.

Desmond lay his head back on the resting headboard of the sofa, his eyes rolling back.

"Pasbrut wasn't nearly as fatal as the news treated it, even at its height. Your throat hardening and piss going bloody was obviously something major to worry about, but it was rare for a person to actually *die* from having it. A healthy person, at least. When my brothers caught it from me, it was a different story altogether," Desmond explained. "Christopher was always the type to get sick easily, so we weren't surprised by how badly it had affected him. And Leon probably would have been fine if he were luckier. We thought he had recovered from it until one day, his cricopharyngeal muscle locked and spasmed whilst he was driving."

The prelude of flooding tears coated Chantelle's eyes, glossing them a brighter hazel. "They both died?" she asked with increased sorrow.

"Yes, they died," Desmond answered, exhaling deeply as he bowed his head. "Christopher passed away in the hospital two weeks after his diagnosis. A week after that, my little sister Mia was in the car with Leon when his spasm occurred, so they both fell victim to the crash. In less than a month, I became an only child."

Slow tears flew from Chantelle's eyes. She sprang forward and clung to him. "You poor thing," she wept as she swallowed him in her warmth, her hand entangled in the curls of his hair as she consoled him with comforting head rubs.

Desmond held her back tighter. He concentrated all his effort on not becoming tearful. He could not allow himself to. Not in front of Chantelle.

"Those few weeks changed my life forever. My parents still haven't forgiven me for causing everything that happened, and I don't blame them," Desmond continued. "I've never been able to move past it myself. I force myself not to think about it most days. But even during the best moments of my life, the memory lingers."

Chantelle kissed him on the forehead. "You're so strong," she whispered, warming his face with both hands on his cheeks. "I can't believe you've been carrying this without telling anyone."

"There's no one I want to tell. I almost regret deciding to tell you," Desmond said.

Chantelle nodded, wholly understanding. "But why were RealSlaek going to use that as blackmail against you?" she asked. "It's not like you meant for any of that to happen! It wasn't your fault! Not in the slightest!"

Desmond shrugged. "Sean MacGowan didn't give me the privilege of finding out how they planned to use that information against me, just that they did," he said. "When he brought it up, I was in too much shock to question it, and I'm not in the mood to ask him about it anytime soon."

Chantelle shook her head in disgust. She drew Desmond in for another love-felt kiss to the forehead. Desmond felt a tingling warmth swim through him.

"We work for a hateful company. We do hateful things for hateful people. But that doesn't mean we can't be as loving to each other as possible," she told him. "If you ever have something that plagues your mind, don't keep it to yourself. Remember that I am here to listen to and support you. I won't be like your parents or anyone else. I'll *never* abandon and *always* forgive you. Always."

The floodgates were about to burst. Desmond was desperate to let out the building tears, but equally as desperate to keep them at bay. He held Chantelle closer, resting his head over her shoulder as she wrapped her arms around him. A single tear escaped from each of his hard-shut eyes.

"I love you," Chantelle whispered.

"I love you, too," Desmond whispered.

***

The following evening was spent in higher spirits as Desmond and Chantelle attended another RSRF employee event. Just as the last event, where Desmond had received awards for his great work, this event was held in the red celebration hall. The same spacious, spectacular room with the star-shaped seating arrangement and the ancient mythological Slaek-adorned statue servants.

Desmond wore a black suit so slick and tailored it shone. Chantelle wore a dress matching in colour, decorated with the onyx stone jewellery and raven roses he bought for her.

The general attendance of employees at the event buzzed with even more excitement than they typically would. His friend Jack and a few others had informed him of the rumours that were spreading around. That some big-time secret RealSlaek investors would be attending the event.

Desmond had heard time and time again of the major investors whom RealSlaek RF acted in the interests of. There were many famous public figures who Desmond knew must have been key investors, but he was yet to get confirmation on a single one of these hunches. That was soon to change.

An hour into the event, one of these investors had shown their face. The most famous one of them all had arrived. The man entered the event to the sound of the wildest round of applause Desmond had ever heard or witnessed. Once Desmond had seen who it was, he realised such an investor deserved such applause one thousand times over.

President Ezra Elbaz had joined their party.

QUESTION, DREAM

THE PRESIDENT. Despite him standing there, right in front of his eyes, casually conversing with RealSlaek employees, Desmond could not believe it. He was attending the same event as *the* Ezra Elbaz.

He was much shorter and slimmer in person than Desmond expected, yet he somehow stood out even more than on video. The man glowed. From his shining navy-blue blazer to his vibrant youthful haircut, his unnaturally unblemished tawny skin, and his ever-present pearly smile. His entire being acted as a bright beacon that drew every attendant's attention towards him.

"President Elbaz!" Sean MacGowan greeted, offering the Renyland leader a handshake. Elbaz's smile stretched wide enough to tear his face.

"MacGowan," he greeted back, rejecting the handshake and pulling him into a hug instead. A gesture that the RSRF head employee laughed at and accepted with gratitude, holding onto him like he was a dear childhood friend. Desmond never knew Sean was capable of such affection.

"I have to say, I'm surprised you came. Even though you insisted you would," Sean said. "I trust a busy man of your stature must have an infinite number of more important places to be at this very moment."

Sean laughed heartily, to which Elbaz reciprocated as if he was challenging him to see who could exude positive emotion the most.

"My schedule was tight, but I had to make time," Elbaz said. "This is my favourite branch after all."

Sean placed a genial arm around his shoulder. The two of them disappeared into the swarming crowds as the RealSlaek analyst showed the president around the event. The Renyland leader was reintroduced to top RSRF employees as well as newly acquainting himself with the fresher crop of recruits.

As he watched him move through the event, Desmond waited for an opening. A chance where he could have a real discussion with the president without getting swarmed. He had to know more about the man he looked up to from the source itself.

***

Desmond could not focus on enjoying the event for himself, his attention somewhat drawn towards President Elbaz's presence in the room at all times.

A lot had surprised him from his observations that night. In the hours that had passed, he had not seen Elbaz make a speech or give a special talk or attempt to capture the crowd in any way one would expect. Throughout the night, he had acted as if he were any other event attendee, mingling and conversing with the people of RealSlaek RF as if he were on their level. Attention came to him regardless. Every time Desmond glanced over at him, up to ten employees were entertaining him, desperate for his undivided attention.

"You can't believe he's here either, right?" Chantelle asked. Desmond's eyes blinked as if he had been snapped out of a trance. He turned back to her, a hint of shame about him.

"I'm guessing you've noticed how much I've been staring his way?" he asked. Chantelle shrugged with a coy smile. Desmond smirked sheepishly.

"You should try to go talk to him," Chantelle suggested. Desmond sighed. "I might," he said. "Not now. Maybe later."

Chantelle chuckled. "I know you admire him. You don't have to pretend to be unconcerned," she said. "I'll find someone else to talk to. In the meantime, meet your idol."

Desmond smiled. He gave Chantelle a kiss on the cheek, making his way to join the crowds of people who had also been seeking out Ezra's attention.

***

"President Elbaz," Desmond called out to him. The president had momentarily split from a swarming crowd to eat. A plate of soft-shell crabs was floated into his hands just as Desmond approached him.

"Hello," Elbaz greeted him with an outstretched hand. Desmond almost stopped himself in his tracks. This was the closest he had ever seen the world leader's flashy, irreverent smile. It prompted goosebumps to rise all over his body.

"Very nice to meet you, sir," Desmond said, shaking his hand with a cheesy grin. He straightened out his face immediately after releasing his hand.

The highest priority on his mind was not to lose himself in fanboy behaviour. He resolved to keep his composure and talk to the president as if he were an equal. He believed that would be the best way to approach conversation.

"I don't believe I've seen your face before. You must be one of the employees from the last graduate batch."

"I am, yes. I've been a RealSlaek RF employee for over half a year now."

"Wonderful. What's your name?"

"Eze. Desmond Eze."

President Elbaz's eyebrows furrowed as his mouth contorted into a half-malevolent, half-delighted smile.

Desmond was unsure as to what emotion was being conveyed and why saying his name had provoked it. The president paused for a while, silently nodding as he flashed a strange smile Desmond's way.

"I have a lot to thank you for, Desmond Eze. If I'm not mistaken, you're the promising young employee who orchestrated the self-directed Slaek-warehouse scheme," he finally said. "And you played a role in both Prime Minister Lange and Tyler Joseph Washington's deaths. Am I correct?"

"Yes," Desmond said with a contained rabid excitement coursing through him. "I'd have never expected you to be so familiar with the work I've done."

"I'm very familiar. Your name is near the top of the list of rising employees here."

"It is?" Desmond asked.

"Smyth, Lindsay, Runqvist, Itagaki, Johnstone, Hartman, Catalado, McEntee, Forster, Khan, Levy, Belle, Dathom, Strafford, Gould, Nguyen, Milner, Proctor, Connors, and Eze," President Elbaz listed. A good showing of that impressive memory of his, which Desmond recalled being used to throw out statistics during political debates. "Those are the names of fresh employees I was told to keep in mind."

Desmond recognised all the surnames that were listed before his. All were the last names of the most successful employees in his age group. A few of them were those at the company he was most heavily acquainted with. It did not

128

surprise him that Chantelle was amongst that list of names, whereas it did surprise him that Margot and Lloyd were.

"Of those twenty names, the three I was most interested in meeting were Levy, Smyth, and you. The other two had already introduced themselves to me much earlier in the night," Elbaz chuckled. "I was starting to worry you wouldn't do the same until now. I'm glad we've finally met, Eze."

Desmond nodded, his body bursting with such bright emotions, yet only able to muster a gasp of disbelief as he looked back at him. Thus far, the conversation was going far better than he could have ever anticipated. Anyone eavesdropping would think the president was the one more excited to see *him*. It gave him the confidence to push the discussion in a direction he thought was risky. He wished to converse on a deeper level.

"Mr Elbaz, is it alright if I ask you a personal question?" Desmond proposed.

The president shifted closer to Desmond, his lips slightly pursed with curiosity. "Go ahead. What is it you *personally* need to know?" he chuckled as he put away his plate.

Desmond lowered his head, coughing to clear the building lump in his throat as he reflected for a few seconds. He raised his head again with boldness, having figured out how he was to phrase his inquiry.

"Ever since I became an RSRF employee, I've struggled with my feelings towards the company and its actions. When I first arrived, I had great disdain for Slaek Devices and a distaste for the company as a whole. Over time, I've learnt to appreciate Slaek and the good it can do for the world, mostly due to following your political career. But I've not been able to completely suppress my distaste for this company. I've only been able to ignore it so I can do my job," Desmond

129

verbally dumped on the world leader. He paused his rant, waiting to gauge Elbaz's reaction midway.

"I see," was all the president muttered, his arms having crossed. He said no more, waiting for Desmond to resume. The young RSRF employee did so with hesitation.

"If I'm allowed to be quite frank, sir, RealSlaek cannot be described as a decent company with decent people. No matter what the heads, employees, and your fellow investors might say, what we do as a company borders on being morally bankrupt," Desmond said. "Some within our own ranks have gone as far as saying we're the evilest company of our time, and I can't help but feel they might be right."

"Interesting perspective," Elbaz said. His voice, which typically possessed a somewhat high-pitched sunny ring to it, was now low and measured. His fixed contemplative eyes made Desmond wary to continue speaking. He found the courage to carry on regardless.

"I know your personal ethos. You want to create a brighter future for Renyland and then the entire world through the use of Slaek. That's why you're our company's top investor. So, I suppose my question is..." Desmond laboured on. "...how can a man like you, a man who constantly acts as a positive force, be so comfortable with what we do to help you build that brighter future? How do you move towards your beautiful dreams when factoring in the disgusting actions taken for them to come true?"

In spite of the regret that shook his soul as soon as the words had left his mouth, Desmond was glad he spoke his mind. He considered that perhaps it would have been better if he had phrased his questions differently. There was a high chance he had offended the president, considering his appearance and body language.

His regrets passed with quickness. He knew he needed to voice these concerns at some point. Better out than in. His skill of disregarding and overlooking the amount of emotional guilt that came with being a RealSlaek employee would limit his effectiveness if it went unchecked. He needed to learn how to cope better. And who better to learn from than the investor whose status was his ultimate goal?

Elbaz's smile returned. "It's a simple matter of conviction, Eze. Confidence in the vision," he said. "My ironclad belief in the inherent righteousness of my actions is what spurs me on every day. It sounds like a cliché, but it's the truth. Any evil I do or have had done in my name is a drop in the bucket compared to the bountiful oceans of good I have done and will do for the world."

Desmond stared, wordless and engrossed in the wisdom he was sure was about to be imparted to him. The Slaek-statues floated two glasses of fine champagne into Elbaz's hands. He passed one to Desmond and drank from the other.

"You said you were against Slaek Devices before joining the company, but you learnt to appreciate them through your own work and watching mine. That's good. That's how you're supposed to feel. Just give it some time. After a few more months, you'll begin to feel the same way about the company as a whole," Elbaz asserted.

"I hope so," Desmond said, taking a drink as he listened. Elbaz finished his champagne in one long sip. He threw the glass into the air. A Slaek-statue activated in the background and floated towards a table before it could shatter on the ground. He grasped Desmond by his empty hand.

"Slaek will change humanity for the better forever. *I* will change humanity for the better, forever. All the work you and the other wonderful employees do helps. It helps me change humanity for the better forever," he assured him with a powerfully held gaze. "Worry not if you don't have the belief now, the more work you do with the company, the further it will develop until one day, you see everything the way I do. Until one day, you're standing with me as a leader of a new and improved world you sacrificed so much to achieve. Then it will all seem more than worth it. Trust me."

Desmond felt a tidal wave of cooling relief wash over him. "Right, sir," he said, finally allowing a passionately excited smile to occupy his face in full effect.

There were times when Desmond thought that the president possessed hidden superhuman powers no one else was aware of. His ability to warm the heart and steady the mind of any individual he spoke to was bizarre. It was even more powerful in person. Following that speech, Desmond felt as if all the uncertainty had been dashed out of his mind by the power of Elbaz's words.

At least, for the time being.

CAPTURE, BLEED

HOMETOWN VISITS. What had once been a regular bi-monthly tradition became a preferably avoided trip. With him still having not talked to Alistair since the warehouse incident, his perpetually full RSRF schedule, and time spent with Chantelle, Desmond had neither the time nor the desire to return to Ivrear. Circumstances made it so he could not avoid doing so forever, as he was drawn back to the area to deal with his property.

He was not required to be in the town for long. There were a myriad of problems with the home he owned there, including a leak, mould, and issues with gas. All he had to do was inspect them himself, call the appropriate parties to fix them, and then leave. Yet even then, he took no chances. He wanted to be in and out of Ivrear as fast as he could.

As soon as he left the house, he bombed down the street and out of the neighbourhood, fast-walking to where he had hidden his company car upon arrival.

Whilst he walked, Desmond thought of what would happen if RealSlaek were caught. It would obviously spell big trouble for all of them and for the image of Slaek Devices to the millions who used them. But who it would be the direst for was the president. Their biggest investor.

He remembered his pleasant conversation with Elbaz at that event in The Hotel a while ago. With hindsight, he was no longer surprised as to why President Elbaz appreciated him so highly. He was involved in the killing of two of the biggest political thorns in his side, Vrelmany Prime Minister Thomas Lange, and future URZ presidential prospect Tyler Washington. Figures from the only two countries that could ever challenge Renyland's international sway had their anti-Slaek sentiments silenced permanently.

Desmond rarely thought back to the late Thomas Lange. But Tyler Washington often came to mind. The young politician was born in the same year as Desmond's eldest brother Leon. Both had passed away well before their time due to his actions.

Any time guilt over the execution entered his mind, his rationale would take over. Comparisons of Washington to a young Elbaz would have previously increased the sympathy he held for him, but as of late, he had seen it in a different light. He had learnt that President Elbaz's involvement with RealSlaek was to such a high level that he possessed greater control over the company than most of the heads there.

Elbaz was not just their wealthiest investor. It was to the point where he could have been considered the real CEO from the shadows. Desmond heard that over half of the highest-level missions were run by him as concepts first before they were even planned. The lovely president was the shot-caller at their 'hateful' company, as Chantelle had referred to it. All of this while keeping up his beautiful public persona of a wonderfully brilliant and altruistic man whose presence drastically improved the world. Although it was not necessarily a persona. Elbaz believed he was exactly that.

A man like Ezra Elbaz was incredibly dangerous, Desmond thought. A man you wanted to have on your side at all costs. A man like Tyler Washington, a budding Ezra Elbaz type with views that clashed against the company, *had* to be disposed of. Desmond decided he was glad he had murdered him. Or else he would have been a problem down the line.

Desmond took a shortcut through a heavily littered side street, still deep in thought. It seemed as if just his thinking about the execution sent shockwaves of bad energy through the universe that were to bounce back towards him.

In a sudden instance, he was captured in a similar way to what he, Margot, and Lloyd had done to Washington. As he turned a corner on this side street, he was ambushed by multiple thugs. They sprang towards him. Before he could as much as gasp in surprise, he had been apprehended by four in white vests and purple masks.

Desmond's first instinct was to fight and scream. He was prevented from doing either. Another masked thug rushed from around the corner, belting him in the face, chest, and stomach with a flurry of hard-knuckled blows. Desmond tasted blood and metal soon after, a sturdy gag being tied around his head and forced into his mouth. The similarities between him and Washington continued as a blindfold was wrapped over his eyes, blackening his vision.

***

When Desmond's blindfold was removed, he recognised where he had been taken. A fact that both relieved and frightened him for many reasons. The five thugs who had ambushed him were still holding him hostage, two pulling back his left arm, two his right, and one keeping his body in

135

a hold. He was in a familiar wooden shack of a house with burnt trash in the corner and no other possessions populating it. It was a discreet den belonging to a childhood friend. A location he fondly remembered smoking weed and flirting with girls in, alongside its owner.

The owner of the den revealed himself, approaching him after he burst the door open. What Desmond dreaded had come to pass. He and Alistair met each other eye to eye for the first time in months.

"You were smart not to show your face in Ivrear for a while," Alistair said. "But you were stupid to think you could rush in and out without shit happening to you."

Alistair punched him across the face, aiming across his eyeline as he delivered the blow. Desmond's eyes watered with sweltering pain as he reeled back from the punch. Alistair smirked with menacing contentment.

"Take that shit out of his mouth," he ordered the thugs who were holding him.

Desmond's metal gag was untied from around his head and removed from his mouth in a revolting drip of saliva as he gasped for air. He was still silent following its removal, disbelief clouding the hundreds of thoughts he wished to verbalise at the moment.

"Alistair?! What's all this?!" Desmond gasped, furious.
Alistair struck Desmond with a backhanded slap. "What the hell have you been doing? Ignoring me! Avoiding me! Blocking my calls and acting like the shadiest prick alive!" he retorted. "That's the question that needs to be answered! Right fucking now!"

Desmond answered. "I'm sorry! I felt guilty about the mission going so badly. About those guys you hired dying. I knew if I contacted you, you'd bring it up, and I haven't been in the mood to talk to you about it!"

"Months, Desmond, months. That shit with the Defrohwe boys goes down, and you ignore my calls for fucking months?!" Alistair exclaimed.

"I've been busy with my job at RealSlaek!" Desmond excused. "It's been a hectic few months! I've barely had time for myself, never mind to check up on *you*!"

Alistair shook his head like a defiant bull. "Nope. That's not it *at all*. Don't fucking lie to me, you slimy cunt."

"Then what the fuck is it, Alistair?!" Desmond asked, an exclamation that earned him another punch. "Ah! Fuck!"

Alistair tapped the side of his head as if the question was crazed. He laughed as if he were a madman.

Desmond recoiled. He could deal with his violent tirades of anger, but not when intertwined with his godforsaken laughter. That was what he could not stand. That meant he was about to see Alistair Armstrong at his worst.

"It's funny you mention your job at RealSlaek. Because I've been thinking a lot about it. Some shit doesn't add up. Or should I say, some shit's starting to add up too much," Alistair said with an angered passion not typical to him. When furious, he often still maintained his boisterous demeanour. But as Desmond listened to him speak, he sounded melancholic, measured, and frayed.

"You've been acting odd since you got a job there. That weird fucking company's definitely doing some weird, creepy shit, and you're definitely playing a part in that fishy, shady, weird, creepy shit."

"Fishy, shady shit? What in the ever-living-fuck are you talking about?!" Desmond asked, faking confusion and ignorance to go along with his genuine exasperation.

"I did some research on that RealCuntSlaekFirm whatever-the-fuck company of yours!" Alistair said, his voice reassuming its usual bombastic cadence. "I read some stuff online, went down a few too many rabbit holes, and heard out a lot of conspiracy theories. Most smelled like bullshit, and any smart person in those threads treated these theories as if they were. But I got a feeling about them."

"A feeling?" Desmond asked.

"A gut feeling! A fucking burning one! No matter how much shit I read about these theories being bullshit, I couldn't shake the feeling that they weren't!" Alistair exclaimed. "A powerful company that blackmails or kills whoever they need to increase the sales and distribution of their devices and shit? To me, that didn't sound too far-fetched!"

Desmond sighed. "You've lost me, Alistair."

He had also read a lot of these conspiracy theories. He was surprised at how accurate a few were. It was almost like it was former employees who were posting them. None of them pointed to any proof that would implicate and expose RealSlaek, nor prompt an investigation into their actions. Not a single one of them. Even if they did, Desmond knew RealSlaek would hunt them down with another gruesome execution mission, especially if they were in fact former employees posting anonymously. Hyper-accurate conspiracy theories did not worry Desmond, nor did the prospect of Alistair learning the truth. All that worried him was that he was still captured at the man's mercy.

"No, I think you understand me just fine. I think you know *all* about Slaek company killings, actually," Alistair insisted. "Especially since I know for a *fact* that you were involved in at least one!"

Desmond laughed. "You should hear yourself now. 'Fucking ridiculous' couldn't possibly begin to describe it," he mocked. "You can't honestly expect me to take any of this shit seriously."

Alistair imitated Desmond's laugh with obnoxious exaggeration, throwing the mockery back in his face. Midway through this song and dance, his face hardened as he resumed his serious interrogation. He moved in close enough for the restrained RealSlaek employee to smell his breath.

"Lie all you want, but I know you had those Defrohwe boys killed and made into a stupid fucking Slaek sob story. That's why you insisted that I didn't send in myself or any of the other Westout boys," Alistair explained. "It's no wonder you changed your mind so quickly. You saw an opportunity to do more shady bidding for your company, didn't ya?"

Desmond deployed another fake, ridiculing laugh. This one was not as convincing as his last few. Alistair did not mock his laugh or even crack a smile. If his goal was to put Desmond on edge, he was passing with flying colours.

Desmond exhaled deeply. "What do you want me to say to that, Alistair?" he asked. "Honestly, what am I supposed to say in response to that mountain of nonsensical horseshit?"

Alistair shook his head. "I never realised how much of a slimy, scheming bastard you were this entire time, mate," he sighed. "I won't miss you much."

"What does that mean?" Desmond asked.

Alistair shrugged. "Yeah, I really won't miss you."

"What does that mean?!" Desmond repeated. "What does that fucking mean, Alistair?!"

The thugs restraining his arms and body held him tighter. Alistair sighed, turning around and walking towards a pile of car parts. He reached behind it to pick something up. He walked back to him with a Glock in hand. Alistair waved the gun in his childhood friend's face, his intentions clear.

"Shit," Desmond gasped.

"See you never, dickhead," Alistair scoffed, his finger hovering over the trigger.

Desmond had frequently wondered what it would feel like to face death, especially since joining RealSlaek. He was curious to see how he would respond. Now that he was in that scenario, he found his response to be an unexpected one.

He did not cry, he did not shout, he did not beg, he did not even calmly plead to be spared. Despite every inch of his inner mind, body, and soul crying for forgiveness and begging God, the universe, and everything in between to save him, his outer self showed no signs of fear. He could only look at Alistair and the gun, dispassionate. A part of him had accepted there was no way out. That any further struggle or panic would be futile and unreasonable. The least he could do was keep his dignity and die shamelessly.

Desmond would not die that day, shameless or not. The begging of his inner mind, body, and soul had been answered by God, the universe, and everything in between in the most catastrophic way.

A gunshot blast echoed through the room, though not the shot everyone had been anticipating. A smoking hole was created in a wall. On the other side, they saw a floating shotgun. The thugs who held Desmond released him, watching the hovering weapon enter the room.

"Who's fucking about with Slaek around here?!" Alistair asked, screaming with rage.

He impulsively fired off a round at the gun, taking the weapon out of the sky. Of all his reckless acts, and Desmond knew there were many, this would go down as the greatest mistake of Alistair Armstrong's entire life.

The empty hole in the wall was filled with carbon steel as ten pistols, shotguns, and rifles replaced the one he had shot down. In one emphatic boom, all fired at once. Countless bullets sank themselves into Alistair's flesh and bone. Most through his face, leaving his mangled mouth hanging by a lip. A good amount were aimed at his legs, exploding his kneecaps and tearing apart his thighs. Three blasted through both arms, one to the hand that held the gun and two to the hand he reflexively tried to protect himself with. Finally, one pierced straight through his heart.

"Fuck!" yelled one of the thugs who had been restraining Desmond.

Every thug endeavoured to make a break for it, for the slight chance they could avoid ending up as Alistair had.

Desmond sat frozen as the army of guns soared through the air, chasing the thugs down. As they turned their backs to run, each one of them was blasted in the spine, stopping their pointless escapes.

RealSlaek employees must have realised Desmond had left Capcounty City and failed to return for a much longer time than he had told them he would that morning.

They sent agents to track him down, agents who came just in time to save him from an execution at the hands of the Westout Street boys. It was inevitable. Alistair might as well have been dead the second he had his thugs grab him.

Desmond ignored the madness and mayhem echoing around him as the thugs were shot and killed in the most creatively sadistic ways possible, all of their bodies reduced to mutilated pulpy messes, bullet after bullet.

He only cared to see Alistair, watching motionlessly as his former best friend bled out.

TORTURE, NUMB

GRIMEY TORTURE. In his seven and a half months of working for RealSlaek RF, Desmond had been no stranger to it. But never before had he been subjected to it.

The RealSlaek employees who tracked him down had taken him to one of the barren, purposeless storage rooms on the bottom floor of The Hotel an hour after he had watched his childhood friend die. There, he experienced what it was like to be on the other side of the pain and questioning.

The RealSlaek agents forced him onto the wall using Slaek Devices, holding him there as they beat his face and body. They ripped out fingernails, forced them back into the opened wounds, and doused him with freezing water. They piled on the torture as they peppered him with questions about whether he had been 'compromised' whilst in Ivrear.

Desmond understood how it looked from their perspective. He had allowed himself to get kidnapped and almost killed by a group of low-level street thugs. An employee of his current status should never have allowed such a pitiful thing to happen to him. Since he had allowed that to happen, who knew what else he had faltered on? From their point of view, it seemed any number of company secrets could have been spilt due to the same incompetence that led to his near-death at the hands of those hoodlums. Understanding why did nothing to ease the abuse he was dealt. Going through this physical and mental torment shortly after seeing Alistair pass before his very eyes made Desmond sure this had to be his single most unpleasant day ever.

Desmond already felt as if he was a shell of who he once was when they had brought him to the room. The torture only succeeded in hollowing him out further. Once the assigned RealSlaek employees had been satisfied, determining that Desmond had not been compromised, they left him a shivering, snivelling mess, grovelling on the concrete floors that were stained with his spilt and dried blood.

It was at that moment that a revelation came to Desmond's mind. They had been taught during their time at RealSlaek that torture was an ineffective method of extracting information. Of all the reasons they would have to torture a target, forcing them to admit information was never one of them. They had already determined he was not compromised, and if he had been compromised, they would have killed him along with Alistair and the rest of the thugs. The true purpose of the torture was punishment for the crime of putting himself in such a shameful situation.

"Clean up after yourself," Lloyd ordered with revulsion as he and the other employees left Desmond in the room.

To Desmond, that had to have been the most painful aspect of this ordeal. That Lloyd Gould was chosen as one of the employees to dole out his torture.

Lloyd did not take any sadistic pleasure in doing so. Not outwardly, at least. Desmond might have preferred sadism to the disgust that Gould showed throughout. The tall, devil-eyed employee made a point of spitting on him as he lay on the floor, making his feelings about the work clear.

Desmond had never felt lower in his life.

***

Numb. Even after multiple weeks had passed by, Desmond felt numb. The positive energy he spent the longest time building up within himself in relation to the company had been sullied by one bad day.

Every time he did a task on behalf of the company, Elbaz's beautiful words about the good work he was helping him do were spoiled by constant reminders of the day he was brutalised. On the rare occasion, it would be the replaying image of Alistair dying in front of him.

It did not help that a part of his punishment following his 'potential compromise' was a temporary month-long demotion that lessened the goodwill his work with the Belle family had given him. This meant he would have to conduct more missions with the likes of Margot, who he promised Chantelle they would both do their best to avoid, and Lloyd, a walking reminder of his day of torture.

Desmond spent another mission flying through the air. He sat in the seating section of a private jet alongside four other RealSlaek employees, all reclining on seats that acted as cream-coloured sunbeds in this spacious first-class club.

Being on a plane hit Desmond with the urge to drink. He would always drink excessively whilst travelling, especially on holiday trips with Chantelle. He almost never did so on missions for fear of losing focus.

This time around, he treated the mission as if it were a holiday, guzzling down as many drinks as he possibly could with one goal in mind. Numbing himself further.

***

Desmond woke up much later, his head spinning and pounding, his body stiff and sluggish, and his goal of

145

numbing himself with alcohol having succeeded for hours. They were still on their mission, still in the private jet, soaring to God knows where.

What Desmond first saw as he rose was Margot's malevolent smile. None of their other mission partners remained in this area of the plane. The plane itself was astonishingly quiet, as if they had disappeared.

He immediately groaned at the sight of Margot, to which she laughed. She lay in the sunbed-seat closest to his, across an isle of gold-plated tables with discarded food and drink. She stared at him, leaning forward with her hands pressed against her face. The young woman had a look in her eyes that told him she had been waiting for him to wake for a while and was dying to tell him something.

"What the hell do you want?" Desmond croaked in pain. Margot giggled. "I've already taken what I want from you."

Desmond sat up in his seat, scowling with his eyes squinted. "Sorry?"

His muscles tensed as Margot stepped out of her seat and approached his. She cleared the table between them, sat on it, and equipped her phone.

"Don't you remember this?" she asked, putting on a video and turning the screen for Desmond to watch.

Desmond sighed in anticipation of whatever nonsense Margot was about to show him.

The video played, and it immediately bothered him. It was a video of him on the private jet from her perspective, one that had to have been filmed hours ago whilst he was at his drunkest. He was laughing and drinking another glass of cognac. From the sounds of Margot's slurred words as she filmed, she had also been drinking at the time.

In the video, Margot flipped the camera, capturing both herself and Desmond as she lowered onto his lap.

"Come here. Now," video Margot ordered Desmond, pulling him by his shirt collar and hovering her lips over his.

"Fuck me, you're fucking sexy," video Desmond chuckled, gripping her buttocks with both of his hands as Margot mounted him.

The pair aggressively made out with each other, kissing in the sloppiest, most slobbering way a couple could for half a minute until the video ended. Desmond's mouth gaped as if he had just been shown a gory horror video.

Margot chortled. "*Fuck me, you're fucking sexy,*" she repeated. "The things alcohol makes you say. So funny."

"That video's fake," Desmond dismissed without a second thought. "You edited that. It's not real."

Margot sighed. "Don't be pathetic, Desmond dear. You know good and well that I didn't have the time or resources to make fake videos whilst we were out here flying. That video's as real as anything."

Desmond groaned, pinching the skin on his forehead. He wondered why his testicles hurt and his tongue tasted of cherry-vomit when he woke up. He rationalised it as being his body crashing due to his heavily inebriated state, not realising it was a result of what he had been doing with Margot whilst in that state. Of all the stupidest vices he could have possibly fallen into, this topped the list. He hated to think of what would happen if Chantelle were to find out about this. Or if she told Mr and Mrs Belle. He could already see himself stuck to the wall of another torture basement.

"You were a good shag to be honest," Margot laughed. "Not as good as Lloyd, though. But don't feel bad about that because you were bigger than he-"

Desmond pounced forward with an outstretched hand, grabbing her neck. For once, he was the one who caught her off guard. Margot's face dropped with shock and fear as Desmond tightened his grip around her throat.

"If you tell anyone else what we did, I'll kill you. If you tell Chantelle of all people, I'll cut off your limbs, blind you, chain you to a pole for days on end, *then* I'll fucking kill you," Desmond threatened, his voice rough and eyes bulging. "Don't take this as a joke in any way. If you do that, if you take the chance and tell Chantelle because you think it'll be funny or whatever the fuck, I'll truly have nothing to lose. I'll have no other *choice* but to kill you. It'll be a long time coming, and I think I'll really fucking enjoy it."

He let go of Margot's throat, allowing her to crash over the table as she gasped for sweet air.

"Fuck's sake! You're always so dramatic!" she groaned. With a delicate finger, she touched the bruise Desmond's hand had formed, wincing at the pain. "I wasn't going to tell anyone shit, Des! I wasn't!"

"Yeah, fucking right. If I hadn't said anything, you would've sent Chantelle that video the second our plane landed," Desmond scoffed.

"I wasn't and I'm not! I was just going to keep those videos for myself! Honest!" Margot exclaimed.

"I don't trust you! Delete all of that shit. Right. Fucking. Now!" Desmond ordered.

Margot obliged. For the next few minutes, Desmond watched over her shoulder as she deleted the numerous clips from her phone, all featuring them kissing, groping, and pleasuring each other. He was naked in far too many of them.

"Is that the only device you have that the videos could be connected to?" Desmond asked. He thought about the feature where media taken by the same account could show up on other devices automatically. "You better delete those too when you get home. I'm warning you."

Margot smiled again. "I will, I will, I promise," she sighed. "Why do you think so lowly of me, Des?"

He glared, not dignifying her with a response. The two of them sat on their opposing sunbed-seats, Margot keeping her eyes on Desmond whilst he tried his damnedest to pretend that she did not exist.

***

An hour later, a small explosion sounded in the background. Desmond thought he was hearing things until he saw smoke from underneath the door to his and Margot's section of the plane. He rose to check what had happened, only for Lloyd to burst the door open from the other side and march in.

"Did you cause that explosion?" Desmond asked.

"Yes."

"Why?!"

"I'm destroying a section of the plane to destroy any suspicions people have about RealSlaek's flight habits," Lloyd answered as he pushed passed him and dove under one of their seats to retrieve an item. "Not that I should be saying this out loud. You should fucking know already."

"Okay, *why* are you doing that?" Desmond asked. "How does this *destroy suspicion*?"

Lloyd ignored him, scoffing as he continued to rifle underneath the seat. As he did so, Desmond thought about the rumours he heard of Lloyd's RealSlaek-held blackmail story. They involved something along the lines of killing former classmates with explosives. He could not understand how RealSlaek trusted him to create and manage controlled explosions, mission or no mission.

149

"What's the plan here, Lloyd?" Desmond asked, irritated.

"Maybe if you weren't so busy drinking, you would have remembered the mission task," Margot chastised. "Maybe if you weren't so busy doing *other things,* too."

Desmond shook his head. He tried to zone out Margot's laughter as he left for the section of the plane where the explosion smoke came from.

MOURN, FORGIVE

DOWNWARD TRAJECTORY. Not long ago, Desmond's life both in and out of RealSlaek was on a constant upward trajectory. By this point in his life, an opposite phenomenon was occurring.

First, Alistair's death, then the gruelling physical torture, then the complications with the explosive air-travel mission, not to mention his drunken fornication with Margot during it. Even with these issues beggaring him daily, there was still more turmoil to come. That morning, he had been contacted by a woman at a hospital.

"Hello, is this Desmond Eze?"

"Yes, it is."

"Hi, Desmond. It's with a heavy heart that we must inform you of your grandmother's passing."

***

Desmond was not a smoker, having only ever smoked four cigarettes in total. As he stood outside the grey column blocks of the hospital's entrance that morning, he found it fitting to have the fifth of his life.

Natural causes, that was how she had died. Peacefully. They planned to move her body to the morgue by the end of the day. According to the doctors, there was nothing that could have been done. It was her time to pass. Desmond did not take this as an excuse not to blame himself. Over the past few months, he had rarely been able to visit her as much as he should. When he received the call that morning, it was the first time he had thought about her in a while. A thought that worsened the pain.

"Life," Desmond sighed, drained by it all. For a while, he had been completely numb. Now he was not, and he hated it.

Desmond sighed, the weight of the world crushing him down. He tilted his head back on the cylindrical block he leaned upon. His eyes closed as he cried softly and quietly.

"Desmond?" the meek voice of a middle-aged woman called out to him.

He lowered his head and opened his eyes to see who had approached him. As he locked eyes with the woman, the cigarette dropped out of his mouth, simmering onto the floor.

"Mum?" Desmond whispered.

He must have been hallucinating. He had to have been. There was not a flame's chance in a freezing snowstorm that his mother was standing right there, calling out to him. The Pasbrut incident years ago, the accidental deaths of his siblings he caused, the event that made his parents swear never to forgive. Those days were the last time he had seen his mother and the last time he thought he ever would. It made more sense for this to be a mirage of his mind than to accept the reality that his mother was speaking to him again.

"Are you alright, Desmond?" she asked with concern. She had aged quite a bit since the last time he saw her, her skin losing its glow with dark circles around her eyes. Regardless, she was just as beautiful as Desmond remembered. Only greatly worn down by life, it seemed.

He tried to force himself to speak, but was unable to. The shock persisted, only subtly easing by the second. His grandmother had died, and her mother had died. That is why she had shown up. It had nothing to do with him. That was what he had told himself. But that did not quite make sense. Would she not have visited at another time? Or waited until she had seen him leave before entering herself? The fact that she did not gave him hope. She had truly sought him out. She must have. For the first time in years, she wanted to face him. He could almost cry.

"Desmond, are you alright-"

"I heard you the first time. I'm fine," Desmond interrupted, his fuse for her shortening already. "Considering everything, I'm doing alright."

Mrs Eze nodded, meekly avoiding eye contact with her son. "I heard you graduated from university as one of the best students in your year group. And that you've got a very good job at a Slaek Device company."

"That's right," Desmond said. He was not sure where she would have heard about any of this without his knowledge. Perhaps a family friend who followed him online.

"You're doing really well. I'm very proud of you," Mrs Eze complimented with a weak smile.

"Thanks," Desmond replied bluntly. He had long desired to hear these words come from her mouth, yet as soon as they graced his ears, he no longer appreciated them.

Mrs Eze took notice of her son's standoffishness. "I mean it, Desmond, I'm very proud of you," she said. "It warms my heart to see my last son thrive and-"

"Is this why you decided to finally speak to me after all these years? Because I've been doing well? Is that your only fucking reason?!" Desmond asked, blurting out in scorn. He

153

had not expected to resort to angry outbursts this early into their conversation.

"No, it's *not* my only reason," his mother said.

"Why decide to face me after all this time, then? Please, enlighten me!" Desmond ordered with furious laughter.

Mrs Eze sniffed roughly, wiping the tears that were escaping her eyes as she looked at her last surviving child.

"My mother died today, Desmond."

"Yes, I'm aware. I'll have you know that *I'm* the only one in the family who has even tried to care for her in the past year or so," he scoffed. His mother sighed with shame.

"I wasn't saying that to get pity from you," Mrs Eze said. "I remembered something she always used to say to me…"

The scorching rage that was rising within Desmond moderated, simmering down as his scowl softened. His grandmother was not able to complete many coherent sentences in her final months. When she did, there was one sentiment she would repeat in as many different ways as she could. One that would always both warm and break his heart.

"…Evelyn, find it in your heart to forgive your son," she said, echoing his late grandmother. "He's a sweet boy. Please forgive him."

Grandma Mary's favourite words. A phrase loaded with enough emotion to make Desmond crumble. He became as shaky and tear-filled as his mother. The two held their gazes together, sharing a moment of sentimentality.

"She said that all the time. It's all she could come out with most days," Desmond said, brushing away a tear as soon as it left an eye.

His mother nodded heartfeltly. "And I never listened, even though I should have. How cruel of a mother am I to abandon and ignore my only son for years?!" Mrs Eze cried.

"I refused to end up like your father. I had to reconnect with you before it was too late."

"My father? What happened to him?" Desmond asked.

Mrs Eze swallowed hard. "He died a year ago. Heart problems. We were still holding that worthless grudge against you for what happened to your siblings, and I was too heartbroken to call you about it," she cried with remorse. "On his deathbed, he told me he wished he had forgiven you. He told me that it was his greatest regret in life. Not being able to see his son again."

"Lord," Desmond sighed, his voice cracking with misery. He outstretched his hands, gesturing for his mum to come hug him. "I'm glad at least you were able to come back. I'm glad you decided you could forgive me."

Mrs Eze shook her head as she dove into her son's arms. "This is wrong!" she cried. "I'm not the one who should have to forgive you. You're the one who has to consider whether I even *deserve* your forgiveness!"

Mrs Eze shook her head more, her tears staining Desmond's RealSlaek blazer. He sighed. "Mum, it's alright, I understand-"

"You didn't mean to cause your sister and brothers' deaths! You made a mistake. I didn't! I *chose* to ignore you all these years. I *chose* to hold a grudge, to blame you for our family's misfortune! I have no right to even look you in the eye or hold you dearly! And yet here I am, doing just that!" Desmond's mum screamed out with profound, soulful tears. She collapsed in her son's arms. "Here you are, having the heart to accept me again!"

Desmond held his mother carefully and gently. He performed the same soothing motion against her hair and back that Chantelle had done for him the one time he was in a similarly emotional state.

"I understand, Mum. But you have to understand that to me, whether you deserve my forgiveness or not doesn't matter," he said. "I may have cursed you out all these years, but it doesn't change what I've always wanted - for my mother to be in my life again."

Mrs Eze laughed with relief in between her tears. "My mother was right. You really are a sweet boy."

Desmond smiled, appreciating those words. They were not true, however. Not to him. Someone like him could never be considered *sweet*. If only she knew even half of what he had done since joining RealSlaek RF.

If only she knew.

KILL, COVER

THE MAGIC FADED. Desmond thought having met President Ezra Elbaz in person, he would become more appreciative of his work. But that could not have been less true. He lay lazily in his apartment, treating his sofa as a bed. His television blared, the news droning on. The Renyland national leader was being commemorated for another one of his countless good deeds.

From what Desmond had gathered in between scrolling on his phone and staring at the ceiling, President Elbaz had helped Vrelmany fund and erect a commemorative statue of the late Thomas Lange and given a heartfelt speech in front of it. He also announced a plan to help fund youth centres in the capital city, since the state of the general community and young people of Vrelmany were the late prime minister's greatest concerns. Throughout his speech, he would pepper in a few mentions of his Slaek-City concepts, in the hopes of convincing the Vrelman public to be more open to the prospect than their previous leader had been.

Elbaz spent the entire week in Vrelmany, honouring the former prime minister's life and death. The same prime minister that he and the Belles had poisoned, a mission that he was sure was ordered by the ever-smiling politician. That was what happened to you when you spoke against Slaek. Or against anything to do with Elbaz in general.

As much as he tried to appreciate Elbaz's greatness as he typically would, that day, he could only see the falsities behind his smiles. The evil behind his altruism.

What changed? He was not sure. He had always known that Elbaz was connected to RealSlaek. It was not hard to see, since half of their most important missions turned out in his favour. Initially, this had done nothing to affect his admiration. Though it seemed to chip away at his psyche until he could no longer deny a touch of disgust.

Perhaps his current life at RealSlaek was to blame, since at that time, it seemed to be rarely pleasant. He had attached the image of RealSlaek to Elbaz, and so the president's image was rotting along with it.

He reckoned it would be a different story if Elbaz were right in front of him. The energy he exuded was too alluring, the words he uttered too inspiring. Desmond remembered feeling his heart twist and drop when Ezra mentioned how, after a while, he will eventually stand with him at the top in the new world he builds. Alongside Smyth, Levy and the other top employees who the president had taken a liking to.

Sitting up on his couch, Desmond wondered if that was what he wanted. For a while, his goal was to climb the ranks and be as successful as Elbaz. But this was a goal he was losing confidence in. Nowadays, he thought of whether it would be smarter to fly under the radar rather than to shine in a place like RealSlaek RF.

Desmond picked his phone from a crevice in the sofa. Chantelle was calling. Most weeks, he and Chantelle would be spending this lackadaisical downtime together. Yet he had not seen much of her for days. Partly due to their schedules being busier, but mostly due to Desmond's guilt over the Margot incident, fearing she would somehow figure out he had slept with her. He answered the call.

"Hello," Desmond said as he picked up.

No response for a while.

"Chantelle?" Desmond said.

For a while longer, the line remained silent. Then, he could hear heavy breathing. Then, tears.

"You need to help me," Chantelle whimpered.

"What's wrong, love?" Desmond asked.

"Come to the place where you learnt my secret. Come quickly," Chantelle cried. She turned off the call.

In the next forty seconds, Desmond made three attempts to call Chantelle back. His call was cancelled every time.

Desmond grunted, turning his phone off as he rushed out the door. From what he understood, by the place you learnt my secret, Chantelle meant the concrete room where she introduced him to her parents. She would be waiting for him there, where something bad had happened.

Desmond gulped. He had no clue what to expect.

***

Desmond walked around the stone curve of the room he had once traversed in anticipation of Chantelle's parental secret, now anticipating another. His mind went to the darkest places when thinking of what could be waiting for him on the other side of the room. He took a few further steps and found Chantelle at the scene of her incident.

"I did something bad," Chantelle cried like a scared child. Her posture was crooked, her body weak. Her beautiful brown skin appeared to be duller. Upon closer inspection, he saw that certain parts were stained a faded red. As if she had been drenched in blood, attempted to clean herself, but failed.

159

Desmond's heart sank to the point he swore he could feel it burning amongst the acid in his stomach. His darkest expectations of what Chantelle could have done were confirmed as his eyes surveyed this part of the concrete room.

Guns with emptied chambers amongst charred rock, dulled knives scattered around pools of drying blood, broken, torn apart Slaek Devices, and the victim of these discarded items lay around them in pieces. There was a pale torso with chequered blade marks over it. A left leg with bullet holes on the inner thighs. A right leg nowhere to be found, though the pile of loose flesh next to the left explained its fate. Two severed arms with bite marks rested in a corner underneath a bloody ring on the wall, a Slaek Device stain. Last of all, he saw the decapitated head of a female with her eyes gouged out and her messy dark-brown hair torn from the scalp.

These were pieces of the grotesquely disfigured, dismembered, and spread-out corpse of Margot Forster.

"Y-, you killed Margot?" Desmond stuttered.
Chantelle nodded, picking at her skin on her fingers as they grew raw. Desmond felt a painful throbbing in his chest as his eyes scanned every single severed body part once more.

"Chantelle. Why did you do this?"

"I found out, love."

"You found out?"

"She told me about how the two of you had sex during one of your missions."

Desmond sighed. Of course, she did. But it did not explain what he was seeing well enough.

He analysed every piece of Margot's scattered corpse once more. To think Chantelle was capable of this. He struggled to maintain eye contact once he looked back at her.

Chantelle noticed the unspoken distress in her boyfriend's shifting eyes, causing the pain in hers to double as she cried.

"I know what you're thinking. *How could my darling Chantelle be capable of all this*?! I'm asking myself the same question. I've never lost control of myself to this extent before!" she exclaimed, trembling.

"How did this happen?" Desmond asked.

Chantelle all but choked on her own breath as she explained.

"We were at a social event in the celebration hall, and she was getting *unreasonably* drunk. Late into the night, she told me about how you two slept together, insisting that I must hear all the details. I didn't believe her, I thought she was just making it up. Provoking me, like you said she likes to do to people. But then she showed me a video on her tablet..."

Desmond pressed hard against the bridge of his nose, sighing as his eyes squinted. He knew he was not being paranoid when he mentioned how the videos Margot filmed could have been automatically shared to other devices. He knew that he should have made sure Margot deleted them from every application once they returned from their mission. If he had followed his gut, her death could have been avoided.

"...I waited until the end of the night, when she was a few drinks away from passing out and everyone else was leaving. I told her to come somewhere private. Somewhere we could have a drink and 'talk about it'. That was yesterday night. I did *this* to her this morning," Chantelle finished. She waved her hand around, gesturing at the scene of her crime as she wailed.

Strangely, Desmond was impressed with her ability to execute this level of visceral violence, almost to the point of feeling proud. Especially since she had not been caught. Yet.

161

"I can't believe she showed you those fucking videos," Desmond sighed. He clasped Chantelle by both her trembling hands and pulled her in close to feel her heartbeat against him. "I'm sorry, Chantelle. I'm so, so, so sorry. I betrayed your trust and our relationship. Though I hope you can forgive me, I won't blame you if you don't."

Chantelle rested her head against his pounding chest. "I don't care about that anymore. You were drunk and going through a difficult time back then with your friend's death and the torture. You made a mistake in a moment of weakness, that's all," she said, sniffling as she held him. "We have more serious matters to worry about anyway."

The two of them held each other in silence, their eyes fixed on all the blood, limbs, and hair surrounding them. The remains of Margot Forster and all the incriminating DNA one could use had to be scrubbed clean. An expert disposal had to be completed with due dispatch before another employee decided they wanted to use one of these rooms.

Desmond's mind purged out all of the grief and anguish that had held it hostage. He forced himself into planning and problem-solving mode.

"First, we'll clean the room and package up Margot's body parts. Then, I'll need you to call your parents and tell them the truth, that you made a grave mistake and someone died. But lie about the mistake you made, say something along the lines of how you organised an unauthorised or off-the-books mission where your partner was gruesomely killed doing something reckless. I'll help you come up with something and corroborate the story," Desmond advised. "Using their power within the company, your parents should agree to dispose of the body without anyone else having to find out that Margot's even dead yet. With the body disposed of, I'll take Margot's phone, break into it, and impersonate her online for a long enough time period that people won't be too freaked out by not seeing her in person for a while. After that, I'll figure out another plan. One that wipes our hands clean and makes it look as if her death was caused by someone else. Does that sound good?"

Chantelle blinked thoughtlessly, staring at Desmond with relief and admiration. "Yes, that's good. That could work out," she sighed, the stress seeping from her body in cold sweats. He could tell his clear-minded suggestions were calming her down, her heartbeat slowing considerably. She wiped down her tear-soaked face.

"I'm sorry I put you in such a predicament."

"It's alright. Everything's going to be fine, okay, love?"

"Okay," Chantelle said. "I love you."

"I love you, too," Desmond said. Though time was of the essence, he allowed her to hug him for a while longer.

Whilst working at RealSlaek, Desmond had so many mixed feelings evoked within him by so many bizarre events, making him never sure of what was appropriate at what moment. Why did he allow himself to feel at peace in his lover's arms when the putrid flesh of the woman she horrifically murdered surrounded them? He did not know.

His life was a strange one.

DISCUSS, SUCCEED

A MEETING WITH ELBAZ. A sentence that startled Desmond the second he heard it. He was to meet with the national president that afternoon in one of RealSlaek RF's hidden sites on the other side of the city. An inconspicuous, boring building that hid many secrets.

Desmond walked down the hall to Elbaz's RealSlaek office with lines of countless armed personnel standing to either side. Suited men with high-tech guns and Slaek Devices fixed on their wrists leaned on every inch of the walls from the corridor to the sides of the door. Desmond felt queasy walking past them and queasier opening the door to the office itself as he stepped into the president's lion's den.

It was a strange office, appearance-wise. Three of the four walls, the two to the side of Elbaz's desk and the one behind him, had enormous wooden wardrobes built in. They caught Desmond's eye due to how much room they took up, as well as the metal locks around each of their handles. At the top of each of the doors, Slaek Devices had been fastened. Devices that were turned on and floating around metal parts and pieces of scrap paper over Elbaz's head, for reasons Desmond could not figure out.

Elbaz sat behind his desk, vacantly staring at the empty countertop in front of him as the metal and paper span over his head. When he realised Desmond had entered the room, his head shot up and his face stretched into a smile. The metal and paper he had been floating with Slaek Devices were removed from over his head and thrown on top of the wardrobe behind him.

"Afternoon, Eze," President Elbaz greeted, his pearly smile shinier than the last time Desmond had seen it in person. He pointed towards the empty seat on the opposite side of the desk.

"Afternoon, Elbaz sir," Desmond greeted back.
He was anxious about this meeting. It showed in the coarseness of his voice. The RealSlaek heads did not wish to tell him why the president wanted to meet.

Sean MacGowan snappily ordered him to "Find out on his own fucking accord."

At the time, Desmond was halfway done with the plan he was working on with the Belles to cover up Chantelle's murder of Margot. Before he had been called in, he was in the middle of making another online post. He was still using his access to Margot's phone to impersonate her, making it seem as if she was still alive for the time being. Had Elbaz found out? Were he and the Belles about to be spectacularly punished for their transgressions? Those were the questions that ran through his thoughts. All would be answered soon.

"Were you told why I asked for you to meet with me today, Eze?" Elbaz asked.

"I wasn't."

"Good. It's very private. What's to be discussed must stay between you and me."

Desmond struggled to read Elbaz's smile. It could have either been a genuine one filled with excitement over whatever they had to discuss, or a fake one luring him into a false sense of security before he tore him apart.

"What is it we need to discuss, sir?" Desmond asked.

"You remember when I gave you that list of the twenty surnames of rising young employees?" Elbaz asked. "And how yours was amongst the three I was most interested in?"

"Yes," Desmond answered, the tension within him alleviating. Smyth and Levy. Those were the other two names that Elbaz had singled out from the list that night.

Elbaz sat up with a sigh. "It wasn't actually a list of brilliant fresh employees I was told to look at," he revealed. "It was a list of my potential successors, with three names at the top. Smyth, Levy, and Eze."

The president's wily smile had contagious properties, altering the mood of the no longer anxiety-riddled Desmond.

"Your successors?!" he asked, dumbfounded.

"Mhm. I need to pick someone from your generation of workers to become the man or woman at the top. Someone I'll prepare over the years to take over my hidden role as the CEO of RealSlaek and turn into a much-needed public face of the company," Elbaz said. "Smyth, Levy and Eze, those are my choices. And if you'd like to know a secret, I've been leaning towards Eze recently."

"What?! Me?! Really?!" Desmond exclaimed. His mouth was as wide open as a small child in a sweet factory.

All notions of flying under the radar at the company were wiped from his mind. He reasoned to himself that any fear about rising in the company was just him coping with his life at the time following the downward trajectory. In an instant, his mind changed. This was a ticket to the top. Now that this ticket had been essentially placed on the table in front of him, he was ready to snatch it as soon as Elbaz gave the word.

"Yes, you. I've spent the last week deciding which of you three is best. Fiona Smyth was the top candidate for a while, but she's recently proven not to have the stomach for it. Raphael Levy was the next one, he's the son of a family friend of a friend and has worked here the longest out of your generation. But I have another role available that will be more his speed," Elbaz explained. "You, Desmond Eze, are my final decision. I want to train you to fill the gap I'll leave once I become too busy to pull the strings from the background. You're the perfect fit to pull the strings from the front."

"Glad to hear it!" Desmond said, breathless with joy.
But in another instant, Desmond's exhilaration disappeared. He stiffened, considering what he had just been told. Something about it did not make sense to him.

Even including his month-long temporary loss in rank following his punishment-torture, Desmond's career at RealSlaek had been filled with high-quality mission completions and near-perfect task records. He knew his work was good, good enough that Elbaz had already heard of him prior to their meeting at the event hall. Even then, the idea that he was to be groomed to take up Ezra's lead overseeing role at RealSlaek in a few years was utterly baffling.

"Even with all the good work I've done, this still comes as a huge surprise to me, sir," Desmond said. "Why out of every single RealSlaek employee of my generation, am I the most fitting candidate in your eyes?"

President Elbaz narrowed said eyes. This was followed by their darting upwards and a scratching of his stubbled chin, as if he had an important thing to say but had forgotten it at a moment's notice. He stood up from his seat, returning his gaze to Desmond. He climbed the seat, then the table, and squatted on the top. His dress shoes scoffed the fine wood on the table, as he leaned over him, eccentric as ever.

As he sat there, staring up at the squatting president and his grinning leer, Desmond had no idea what he was to do or say in response.

"As I answer that, would you like to know a little about a lot of my childhood?" Elbaz asked out of the blue.

"Yeah," Desmond answered, uncertain. Elbaz giggled, squatting lower as he held his hands together.

"When I was a boy, my family struggled financially, emotionally, and wholly. My mother died in the very early days of my tale. From then on, I was raised by my father and his only friend, Noah. Both were very young men, and neither had the faintest clue of how to raise a child. Not a favourable upbringing, I can assure you," he began. "It wasn't just the fact that they were incompetent in their attempts to bring up the budding young genius I was becoming. It was that they couldn't hide how much they disliked doing it. Noah wasn't malicious. Aside from a few somewhat creepy instances here and there, he was indifferent towards me. My father, however? He only raised me out of duty and not love, for he had no love to give. He hated me. I learned later on in life that it was because, apparently, I, little baby Ezra, killed my own mother by coming into the world."

Desmond listened with a hand resting against his jaw as he leaned on his seat arm. He failed to see its relevance, yet kept quiet, intrigued by the story nonetheless.

"It certainly wasn't intentional. How could it be? I was a *little bairn*. But a bairn whose horrid birth caused many complications that his mother could barely survive, and a series of ailments she could definitely not survive. We found that out just a week after I was born," Elbaz explained. "My father would have been the first to admit his dislike of me wasn't rational, it never is with these things. Where else would he place his grief and resentment but onto its product? The love of his life was dead, and it was all little Ezra's fault."

Desmond shook his head in disgust. "If you don't mind me saying, sir, your father sounds very stupidly immature," he said, surprised by his boldness. "You shouldn't pile those negative emotions onto a child."

Elbaz's smile brightened. "Yes, very true, I'm glad you see it that way, Eze. Anyhow, let me move on with the tale of my life," he continued, stretching out of his squat position and sitting on the desk with a planted backside.

"Go ahead," Desmond said, waving his hand somewhat mockingly as he grew more comfortable with the leader.

Elbaz laughed. "By the time I was eleven years old, I was aware of my father's lack of love for me and gave up on making him change his opinion. I searched for appreciation elsewhere, as unloved children do. It turned out that other kids and adults found it much easier to love me. I found out that the rest of the world outside my house thought I was sweet, smart, exceptionally talented, effortlessly charming, highly capable, and brilliant overall," he recalled with a fond smirk. "My *family* might have resented me, but everyone else was convinced I was destined for greatness. I had always implicitly known this, but was yet to act. That changed. A fire was lit under me, and I was spurred on for the rest of my life. It's how I became the Renaissance man and leader of the Western world I am today."

Desmond absorbed the information. The politician sat quiet, unmoving as he flashed a toothy smile, waiting for feedback. Desmond took a breath. He measured his words before responding.

"You had a very black and white childhood. To experience an abundance of love from the world but a lack of love from those closest to you is bound to have an interesting effect on anyone. It's no wonder you're considered such an intriguing figure. No wonder you've been able to do everything you've done."

Elbaz held his head high in appreciation. "Has that answered your question?"

"I'll be honest, sir. I think I might have a fair idea, but I'm not sure," Desmond admitted.

"Alright, well, think of it this way. Based on that snippet of my life story, how would you describe me in a few sentences?" Elbaz asked.

"A man who used a combination of the alienation and admiration he received in his early years to become not only a very successful person, but the most powerful leader in the world," Desmond answered without missing a beat.

"That's right. But I wanted you to be more specific."

"Specific?"

Elbaz tilted his head sideways. "I am a man who, at some point in his life, accidentally caused the disease and death of a family member, leading to a lack of love from my parental figures, leading to a desire to achieve great success to get that appreciation elsewhere. I'm a young, handsome, dark-skinned, well-dressed man, who got himself involved with RealSlaek in a way that could take me to the top," Elbaz described with a presumptuous smile. "A very specific but fitting description. One that should be very familiar to you. Does it sound like anyone else you might know?"

Desmond's eyebrows raised in acknowledgement. He exhaled a realising sigh. "It sounds just like me," he answered with a stiff smirk.

President Elbaz gave him a somewhat condescending round of applause. "There's your answer, Mr Eze! *That* is why you have been chosen as my future successor!" he announced with joy. "I read the files of all the top young employees. I read every single detail we have on your life from your school years to the unfortunate Pasbrut deaths of your siblings to the study files of your behaviour during your most recent RealSlaek missions. And whilst I was reading, all I could think was - This. Is. Elbaz!"

The president was standing on the table yet again, his eyes a haze as if he was entranced by his own words. Desmond's stiff smile faltered. Somehow, this reveal left him even less excited about his future prospects.

"That's your reasoning? Because our lives share a few coincidental similarities?" Desmond asked, sounding disappointed. "Doesn't sound very solid to me."

Elbaz shook his head with intense disagreement as he jumped off the table. He sat himself in his seat normally for the first time in a while. Desmond's comfortable disposition began to tighten once more as Elbaz glowered.

"Throughout my years as a politician, I've developed a kind of *cult magnetism*. With my fantastic skills, endless accolades, and charitable altruism, there are many who consider me akin to a god-like angel who can do no wrong. But that picture I painted is starting to tear," Elbaz explained earnestly. "Too many people are asking the right questions. Too many people are researching my every action. Some are figuring out my true essence. I cannot afford to let this happen with all I have prepared. I need to fast-track my plans whilst

I'm still at the height of my power. And I need a contingency in case anything unforeseen happens."

Desmond clenched as he listened to the world leader's buttery-voiced diatribe. This was the longest he had seen the president go without springing a smile. Everything he was saying had none of his usual irreverence and was marked by the utmost solemnity.

"You must understand that I'm nearing the endgame of phase one when it comes to my plans for the widespread acceptance of the Slaek-City," Elbaz added. "There are many other phases to come, but this first one is the most crucial of them all. If it's completed, I'm still not in the clear. I'll need to keep track of my plans over the years and make sure someone else can carry out my will if need be. And I'll still need the contingency in case I'm either exposed, killed, or forced to give up my dream in some way. You are the contingency, Desmond Eze."

"Okay," Desmond said.

It was too much to take in such a short amount of time. A thumping knot formed in his heart, twisting and eager to burst out of his chest. Though the room was cold, he could feel the emergence of sweat collecting and beading down his forehead. He had to clench his body tighter to prevent himself from physically shaking.

President Elbaz clenched his fists as he glared at him. He unnerved him more with intense eye contact.

"I already made up my mind a while ago. I'm not *asking* you to be my successor, I'm telling you that you *will be*," he asserted. "The only real question I'm asking is, can I trust you'll measure up when the time comes?"

Desmond hesitated, quite reluctant to respond despite knowing well what his answer was to be. The answer he was always going to give, no matter how much he downplayed it.

"You can," he said with emphatic certainty.

FIGHT, DISPOSE

PANICKED CALLS. They were all Desmond expected whenever he saw Chantelle's name on his phone. Bothersome, but he could not necessarily blame her. He promised to complete the second part of a plan that was set to make sure no one would ever find out she killed Margot. A plan that would make sure they would both never face the excruciating consequences of murdering a fellow RSRF employee and covering it up.

Chantelle completed her part, telling her parents the concocted lie about her 'unauthorised off-the-books mission' and convincing them to help dispose of the body discreetly. They had also helped constantly manipulate the camera footage around both of their living areas and would keep on doing so until Desmond was done with his part. Desmond was yet to complete it. He was yet to enact the plan that would put him and Chantelle in the clear.

It was the worst possible time for this to be a problem he needed to solve. Why did this have to occur around the same time he had been told he was to be Ezra Elbaz's RealSlaek successor? News that would rattle even the most sound of men. To simultaneously deal with both major events was putting his head in a permanent state of unrest.

"Are you sure you have everything figured out?" Chantelle asked, her worrisome voice burrowing into Desmond's ear over the line.

"Yes, Chantelle," Desmond sighed, slowly scaling the staircase that led to his hotel apartment.

"Can you at least tell me what you're going to do?"

"No, Chantelle. It's better if we just let it play out."

"Waiting in the dark on this is making me feel uneasy."

"Don't worry about it. I'll make sure everything turns out fine," Desmond assured as he reached the top of the staircase. He leaned his head against the door, too tired to move.

"Alright, I'll try not to worry," Chantelle sighed.

"Don't, please."

"But you must tell me as soon as everything's about to be done, okay?"

"I will, Chantelle."

"You promise?"

"I promise."

"Good."

"Yes, good."

"Love you."

"Love you."

The call ended.

"Lord," Desmond sighed, groaning as he rested his head against the door. It took what felt like a century for him to take his keys out of his pocket and use them to open the door. The young RSRF employee was the image of lethargy.

Desmond swung the door open, ready to stroll into the room and crash on his sofa. Though he would not be allowed to take the well-needed rest he wanted as he entered his home. Another problem was waiting for him in there.

"What the fuck is that?" Desmond muttered out loud as he looked towards a vent in the corner of his ceiling.

A revolting substance was seeping through the crevices and splattering onto the floor. Desmond walked away from the open door and towards the corner of the living room where it was dropping down, staining a new carpet. A bile-like substance of a thick viscosity that smelled of a godless mixture of low-grade marijuana and animal faeces.

Desmond observed the substance with pinched fingers over his nostrils. He did not know why this was happening or how he was to fix it. Especially not when smoke started to rise off the crude pile.

If Desmond's attention had not been so engrossed by the vent-leaked substance pile, he would have heard the sound of swift footsteps racing up the staircase. By the time he heard these footsteps, he turned around to see that the racing intruder had already rushed into his open door and was coming directly for him. With a Slaek Device around one hand and a baton grasped within the other, Lloyd Gould sprinted at Desmond, ready to attack.

"YOU'RE GONNA DIE!" Lloyd shouted at the top of his lungs, swinging his baton in an attempt to take Desmond's head clean off. Desmond dodged the blow with a duck, only for Lloyd to strike his knee into his chin.

"What the fuck, Lloyd?!" Desmond exclaimed as he fell to the floor, his chin blazing with pain.

On the positive side, the blow had woken him. He could no longer afford to tiredly meander around as Lloyd attacked him with determination. He stood and avoided another strike to the head, but fell victim to a wallop to the chest, making him lose his breath for a moment. He coughed away the pain as he avoided a few more.

"Stand still so I can bludgeon you to fucking death! It's what you damn deserve!" Lloyd shouted.

Desmond raised both his arms over his head to protect his skull. Arms that Lloyd bruised as he brought the nightstick down on them like a hammer.

"What do you think you're doing?!" Desmond exclaimed. For the first time in their bout, he was able to knock Lloyd's baton hand away. He used the opening to get a single strike in. A punch to the face that disoriented the glacier-eyed man for a second until he continued his assault.

"Margot's been missing for a while, hasn't she? No one knows where she's gone. But you do. And so do I!" Lloyd explained between sweeping baton swings. "You killed her! You bloody killed her! I know you did!"

Desmond ran across the living room and jumped over the couch. With a strong push-kick, he knocked the furniture towards Lloyd, hoping to trip him. Lloyd used his Slaek Device to move the sofa with a dismissive wave, shoving it to the side before it could touch him. Two lunging steps forward, and he was right back to beating on Desmond.

"*I* killed Margot?! Me?! Are you being for real right now?!" Desmond asked, feigning disbelief.

Lloyd struck Desmond with swift, successive, unavoidable attacks to both of his shoulders. He made another try for a strike against Desmond's head but missed, his target darting out of its path. He was determined to land that specific hit eventually. A solid hit to the head or face.

"I might not have proof, but I know a murder cover-up when I see one!" Lloyd shouted. "Margot disappears, then starts making strange posts online?! I'm not believing that for a fucking second!"

Desmond backed away from Lloyd, being cornered into his kitchen as he dashed past the island.

"Right, let's say, for the sake of argument, Margot *has* been killed. Why the fuck would I do it?! She's my friend!" he defended himself. "I've known her for years! Since we were both eighteen! We went to the same university and graduated at the top of our class together! She helped me settle into this job and even lived in this apartment from time to time! Why the fuck would *I* kill her?!"

As he explained himself, Desmond hit Lloyd. He grabbed his baton-wielding arm and held him in place long enough to land a right hook to the jaw. Lloyd's head kicked back from the punch. He laughed the pain off.

"She was going to sabotage your relationship with Chantelle Belle, wasn't she?!" Lloyd exclaimed. "I overheard you two on the plane. It explains everything! You killed her because of those videos!"

He gave Desmond a kick to the stomach, causing him to fall backwards and crash onto the island. Lloyd smirked with a deranged, twitching smile, blood staining his lips.

"You've gone insane! Absolutely off the deep end!" Desmond shouted, feigning disbelief again. "Use your fucking brain, Lloyd! There's probably a good reason why she's missing! She's probably just skipping work for a while or gone on a spontaneous holiday adventure without telling anyone! You know how she is!"

"Nope. *You're* to blame, Eze," Lloyd grunted.
Desmond groaned. "Of *all* the potential reasons for her absence, how is me having murdered her the one you're going with?!" he shouted. "Have you not come up with a single other plausible theory?!"

Lloyd shook his head in the slow and measured manner of a crazed man with strong convictions. "There's not a single thing you can say to change my mind or convince me otherwise," he asserted. "You killed Margot, so I'm going to kill you. Simple."

Lloyd twisted his arm, the Slaek Device around his wrist whirring. Desmond's head shifted in the direction of his pantry. Each drawer swung open, including the one where all the meat and bread knives were kept. The blades shook, clanged, and rose out of their containment.

"Oh my God!" he exclaimed.

Desmond dodged one, then two, then three, then four. The knives kept coming his way. Lloyd's Slaek curved one of the knives that had missed Desmond so that it changed trajectory and came back after him. Desmond ducked out of its way and leapt over the island, escaping the kitchen. The curving blades followed him, Lloyd using them as homing missiles as Desmond desperately sprinted around the area.

The flying knives pierced through his home, destroying the walls, breaking the TV, and cutting apart the pictures that hung around it. Desmond ran fast and hard, his mouth tasting of blood and his lungs about to collapse as the knives chased him all over his apartment.

With impressive reflexes, Desmond stepped behind the open door to the flat's corridor. Had he been a second too slow, every single Slaek-controlled knife would have pierced him. Instead, they embedded themselves into the door.

Desmond crouched down low as he hid behind the door, waiting for the sound of stabbing blades to stop and Lloyd's footsteps to continue. The door swung open, with three more Slaek-controlled knives and Lloyd's baton swinging his way.

Desmond rolled out of harm's way, speedily picking up one of the knives in the same motion. He stood up to face Lloyd.

As soon as Desmond was upright, Lloyd finally managed to strike him in the face. He had thrown the baton hard, which Desmond tried to dodge. But he was too slow to, getting himself cracked against the cheek by the solid weapon.

Lloyd laughed as he retrieved his baton. Desmond spat blood out of his mouth, reeling his head back and lunging forward for a counterattack.

Desmond allowed Lloyd to hit him with the baton, not making any effort to dodge as Lloyd swung it at his bicep. Desmond gritted his teeth and bore the pain as he took the opportunity to cut at Lloyd with his knife before his opponent could step back again. He cut wound after wound around the wrist area of Lloyd's arm. Lloyd dropped the baton, using the now free hand to clutch at the wounds. Desmond kept cutting his damaged hand until he saw the opportunity to grab Lloyd's Slaek Device.

What ensued was a long struggle between the two men as they rolled through the apartment's corridor, Desmond desperate to take the Slaek Device off and Lloyd desperate to keep it on. After the endless struggle, which left both parties bloody, bruised, and breathless, Desmond prevailed.

He removed the Slaek Device from his opponent's hand and applied it to his own, tightening it around his wrist and activating it to his will with a strong twist.

"Fuck," Lloyd grunted through blood-soaked teeth. He watched helplessly as his Slaek Device was used against him.

A door at the end of the apartment's corridor smashed open due to a sideways thrusting of Desmond's fist. He curled his fingers, the Slaek Device causing chaos in his bedroom. Five items zipped out of his room at breakneck speeds, with

Lloyd having to duck as they flew to Desmond. He looked up to see the balance of power shift.

"Shit!" Lloyd complained, looking at the five Slaek Devices that floated around Desmond.

Desmond controlled the Slaek Devices, manipulating them until they were all on his person. Two devices joined the one he had stolen from Lloyd, fastening onto one hand. The other three devices placed themselves on the other hand. With adorned forearms of pure magnetic power, Desmond held Lloyd at Slaek-point.

"Try beating me now," Desmond urged him. Any attack Lloyd could think of would be ultimately futile in the face of his telekinetic power.

Lloyd dug his nails into the hair of his lowering head. He sighed with defeat. "Go on. Kill me like you fucking killed Margot, you stupid prick!" he goaded.

Desmond chuckled. "You know what's funny? I was telling the truth. I didn't actually kill Margot," he said. "I *did* have something to do with her death, though. And I'm covering it up. You get half marks."

"Fuck you!" Lloyd screamed, spraying the blood from his mouth all over his body in the process.

A hilarious sight, Desmond thought. "You're the one who's fucked, mate," he mocked.

Lloyd flinched as he heard the activation noises from the Slaek Devices he was being threatened with. Desmond whistled to himself as he floated more items out of his room. Lloyd watched as a pen and a small stack of paper were placed in front of him.

"Here, bro," Desmond said, gesturing down at the items.

"What the fuck is this?" Lloyd asked.

"You are going to write a suicide/confession note," Desmond told him. "I'm going to dictate a story about how you were sleeping with Margot, which is true, and you're going to add in parts about how you wanted a relationship, but she used you, discarded you, and broke your heart into too many pieces to count when you found out she was sleeping with other guys. You're going to write about how this led to obsession, killing her out of fury, your decision to admit you tried to cover up her death, and your guilt-caused suicide," he explained.

"None of that's going to happen," Lloyd said.
He scoffed arrogantly, but he was clearly tense and uncontrollably trembling.

"It's going to happen," Desmond asserted. "After you've written it, I'll put more bloody cuts on both of your wrists, shoot you through the bottom of your chin with a pistol, and leave you in a cellar with the note right next to your corpse."

Lloyd seethed with powerless frustration. He clenched his jaw so violently that the muscles in his neck protruded and his face flushed a bright red. He looked a mess of frothing grunts and swollen veins.

"Just go ahead and kill me now, then. Because I'm not writing shit! Not a single fucking word!" he bellowed. His final act of defiance. Desmond tutted at him.

"Would you like to live your life castrated and blind? With your torn testicles stapled over your eyeless sockets?"

"What?!"

"I'm not bluffing. I'll do it. I'll do exactly that. You'll be blind, bollock-eyed, as well as fingerless and toeless. I'll make you a mutilated fucking freak show!" Desmond threatened. "Would you like that, Lloyd? Is that what you want? Because it's what you're going to fucking get if you don't start goddamn writing!"

Lloyd craned his head, swallowing hard. Desmond could almost hear his thoughts, weighing the two options, listing out the pros and cons of both his awful paths.

Be framed for a murder and die quickly, or be forced to live life as a limbless, castrated, blind freakshow with testicles for eyes? A peculiar set of choices. It did not take him long to come to a definitive answer.

Desmond watched with careful anticipation. He felt his body fill with intense elation as he saw his victim give in, picking up the pen with jittering hands.

"That's what I thought," Desmond scoffed. "Write a nice, believable story so I can dispose of you peacefully."

There were two forces within Desmond at that moment. One enjoyed the sweet vengeance. His sadistic side. The other was disgusted, finding he had become beyond reprehensible. His moral side, a side that had lost strength during his time at RealSlaek. The sadistic side was winning.

Desmond lorded over his formerly violent rival, finding himself to be oddly aroused as he watched Lloyd struggle to suppress his tears and write the note.

PROTEST, LIE

DESENSITISATION. Desmond had grown used to seeing death on a mass scale. He had seen enough people die in front of his eyes for three lifetimes and was no longer as shocked as he was the first few times around.

Even with this inner hardening, there were still instances in which a morsel of the dread and disgust a normal person would feel came to him. They came to him as he looked down from a balcony on high.

The reason why Desmond felt troubled once again at the sight of dead bodies was due to how much he could relate to them. The victims of the massacre that had just played out in front of him were university students, young men and women who looked just like he had on that graduation stage a year prior. Their scarred, lifeless faces reminded him of his before he started his work at RealSlaek.

These piles of student corpses scattered across the city streets were the result of Desmond Eze's most recent self-directed mission. A Slaek protest had erupted within the streets of Lavintonna, the capital city of the United Regions of Zereneva. Pro-Slaek and anti-Slaek student protestors had clashed, occupying the city centre in a collision of maroon and navy URZ flags, 'No to Slaek Devices' signs, commemorative images of the late Tyler Washington, and whatever blunt-force weapons they could risk being caught with should the police break up their protests.

Unfortunately for these URZ college students, before the police could suppress the protests, RealSlaek arrived. With Desmond as the puppet-master, undercover RealSlaek employees were placed all over the city, intentionally exacerbating the protests until they resembled full-blown violent riots. They made sure there were many casualties, most on the anti-Slaek side, of course.

Desmond gave the anti-Slaek protestors ironic mass deaths, using a powerful Slaek Device to tear the roads below them, increasing the carnage that took place as the factions fought, and giving the pro-Slaek side the upper hand.

Desmond and his mission partners made sure that there were enough casualties on the pro-Slaek side to not raise suspicion. Approximately two hundred and twenty-five Zerenevan students died in the streets that day. Desmond knew the mission could not have possibly gone better.

***

Weeks after the URZ mission, Desmond sat on his apartment kitchen island. He read a news article on his tablet, which featured President Ezra Elbaz's quoted thoughts on the tragedy that occurred at the protests.

Most were the usual platitudes he gave after a Western world tragedy. About how sad or shocking the event was and how Renyland would band together with the nation, this time Zereneva, to help *support them through trying times* and *offer aid to ease the burden of pain on their people*. Also, the Renyland president wasted no time in tying the tragedy back to his Slaek-City concepts. With a few statistics and 'personal anecdotes from concerned citizens', he managed to frame

Slaek-Cities in a way that made them seem like the answer to such protests. He diagnosed the cause of the protests as being hysteria over the dangers of Slaek Devices as well as the class divide that came with those with great access to Slaek and those with little.

After dispelling talk of the environmental issues Slaek was accused of causing, he brought up how Slaek-City-Grids would solve most of these issues by providing permanent Slaek use to all that lived in them, with an underground bio-friendly grid that mitigates harm. He promised to build one of the first ever Slaek-Cities in Lavintonna to honour the poor students who died during the riots.

Desmond derived morbid amusement from reading the quotes with the knowledge that he was assigned the URZ protest mission by the very same man who spouted them. Not just that he approved and oversaw parts of it, but that Elbaz himself had *personally* asked Desmond to complete that specific mission at that specific time.

Desmond put his tablet down. He lay there doing nothing, staring into space as he sought to take a break from staring at screens. He looked around his apartment, the front room, the living room, and the kitchen. They were clean, organised, and spotless. You would not know that a while ago, Desmond had the fight of his life here against the late Lloyd Gould.

After Lloyd had written the letter, Desmond held him down as he used a knife to give him multiple wounds that would look like self-harm. He then shot him through the bottom of his chin using a pistol with a heavy silencer. He called Chantelle, who helped him transport Lloyd's corpse in a rolled-up carpet wrapped inside a bin bag. They used a hardly-travelled route towards the Hotel cellars at a time of the night when most employees were either sleeping or on missions. They placed the body there along with the suicide note before it could be seen.

Chantelle was happy to oblige, grateful that Desmond had finally come up with a plan to sort out the entire Margot-murder cover-up ordeal. They had spent the next week involved in the gruelling process of cleaning Desmond's apartment and replacing the broken items. Whenever they were asked how Desmond's apartment had become so thoroughly destroyed in the first place, Desmond would pretend to be sheepish and spin a fake story about him and Chantelle having constant rough and violent experimental sexual escapades. A simultaneous pride-and-shame-inducing story that Chantelle corroborated, naturally. One that was believable considering the noise complaints the pair had gotten from their *real* sexual escapades in the past.

Four days later, Lloyd's dead body was found in the cellar along with the suicide/confession note and the series of Margot's belongings that Desmond had taken off her body, including her phone. RealSlaek RF did not investigate any further, the company deeming the 'Missing Margot Mystery' to have been solved.

Desmond remembered still feeling constantly tired for weeks after it had all subsided. He was glad to have put that ordeal behind him. Just thinking back on it was exhausting, prompting him to sleep there on the kitchen counters.

***

Desmond sat across from President Elbaz in his claustrophobic office at the hidden grey-site building. The president was using the Slaek Devices on his wardrobes to float miscellaneous scrap items through the air again. A practice that, whenever Desmond asked about it, Elbaz would laugh in response and promptly continue with whatever conversation they were having before it had been brought up.

"What was it you wanted to ask me before we ran out of time last meeting?" Elbaz said to him this day. "You said it might lead to a longer conversation that needed to be had?"

"I did," Desmond said, tracking his mind for the question. "That's right, I wanted to ask you about the first phase. The Slaek-City concepts."

Ezra giggled, pleased by the chance to talk his mouth numb about Slaek-Cities. "What did you want to know?"

"Do you believe in them?"

"Do I believe they'll work? Definitely. I've worked closely with top-level Slaek engineers who can make sure they run smoothly."

"No, I meant, do you believe in them in essence?"

"In essence?"

"The things you say on television. What you tell the world about how Slaek-Cities will solve every societal problem. Is that true?"

"Oh, right. You're asking whether I believe the claims I make about how, for example, Slaek-Cities will provide an easily accessible and traversable vibrant community for those moved into them?"

"Yes, exactly."

"Then yes. I do believe what I say on television. Though perhaps not in the way you're suggesting."

Desmond appeared displeased with this answer, his brow lowered into a wary frown. "What does that mean?"

President Elbaz pursed his lips. He was briefly distracted by the floating scraps of metal and paper around his office, refocusing once he grew tired of watching them.

"Scratch what I said before. What I meant was, yes, I believe that Slaek-Cities will improve people's lives. But no, I don't believe they will in the specific ways I mention on TV," Elbaz answered with a casual shrug.

"The stats and stories you use to convince the general public are lies?" Desmond asked.

"Well, I take real statistics and I twist and reinterpret them to fit my purposes. I take real stories and I edit them to fit as further proof of those statistics."

"Right, so if those statistics and the 'citizen anecdotes' you supplement them with are somewhat false, what are the *real* reasons as to why you think Slaek-Cities will improve the lives of the people?"

Elbaz gazed past Desmond and towards the office door behind him. His eyes traversed every inch of the door, making sure it was locked and undisturbed. Satisfied, he faced Desmond with a grin.

"I'll let you in on a cheeky secret. You might be told differently, but most people shouldn't be free. They don't have the competence or will to guide themselves, and they can't be trusted to act properly without constant guidance," Elbaz explained. "My Slaek-Cities are going to be constantly surveilled and highly regulated with hidden miniature cameras and tampered remote-control Slaek throughout the grids. Forget committing crimes, a citizen will hardly be able to fart in the wrong direction of the wind without being seen and subsequently dealt with. I'll make sure of that. The more Slaek-Cities built, the more of these observable bubbles that can be created. Therefore, more of humanity will be kept safe and secure, allowing me or whoever is in charge to always watch over them and manage it all with ease."

"I see," Desmond said, nodding with comprehension.

What he understood was that if Slaek-Cities were to become commonplace in the future, it was crucial he made sure that neither he nor anyone he cared about lived in one. Living there sounded like an unbearable existence, though he would never voice such an opinion to President Elbaz.

"Anyway, as I've said before, Eze, that is only phase one of many, many, many."

"Oh yes, that's right. There are multiple phases to your grand Slaek vision."

"Many more phases, many more years to enact them. That's why we need to get to work."

"What's the next phase after this one?"

"Don't ask. You'll find out later."

"When?"

"After I've officially tested you. If you pass the test, I'll brief you on every single phase."

"I'm to be tested?" Desmond asked with concerned curiosity. "What will this 'test' entail?"

Ezra looked away from Desmond, his eyes to the sky as he daydreamed. "You'll see," he giggled like a schoolboy.

Desmond sighed. The president's impish laughter struck him as a bad omen.

RELAX, REFLECT

REAL RELAXATION. Desmond could not remember the last time he had truly achieved such a state. The days in which he would sit on his sofa hardly counted, as he would spend most of this relaxation time reading articles, aligning his schedule, and completing other low-level yet stress-inducing pieces of preparation for his next mission. Even those days were becoming sparser. He considered himself lucky to even get the chance to sit on his own sofa as of late.

Desmond returned to The Hotel following another intense international mission with the goal in mind of fast-tracking Phase One: *Large-Scale Slaek-City Acceptance.* There was still much more work for him to do on that front. These were the list of missions Desmond would see himself having to complete in the next month or so:

1. Bribe a series of rising Renyland politicians, convincing them to spread the good word about Slaek-Cities and incorporate them somehow in their policy manifestos. Afterwards, his focus would have to be on those in countries on the continent of Evincop that were partial to Renyland.

2. Travel towards the first prototype Slaek-City in a secluded island nation overseas, film footage of how well it

is going and have it 'accidentally' leaked to some journalists. A lot of editing and cutting around would have to be done to hide the budding disaster it was becoming, so that those who watched the video would keep faith in the 'bright future' Elbaz promised with these concepts.

3. Apply pressure on a group of Schvanish scientists, making them leak falsified studies that reveal the 'recently discovered unknown health benefits' of regular Slaek usage. Among these, clear skin and a clearer mind were included.

4. Collect information on and screen Karl James Peters, the recently elected Prime Minister of Vrelmany. He was taking over from the slew of temporary leaders they had been cycling through in the wake of Lange's demise and the instability it caused the nation. RealSlaek needed to ensure he had pro-Slaek stances, unlike his predecessor.

5. Kickstart another set of URZ Slaek-oriented protests, this time in Acrubusnon, the biggest city on the opposite coast to Lavintonna. This time, he was ordered to make sure that instead of an even massacre with slightly more anti-Slaek protestors dying, they should make sure it results in an anti-Slaek victory, with the vast majority of the victims being on the pro-Slaek side. It would help build the new narrative they needed in the next news cycle.

6. Follow up on the lead with the Evincopan politicians. Find out if they are willing to 'play ball' with RealSlaek. If not, release the scandalous pieces of information collected for a few of them from last month's mission in order to strike fear into the hearts of the others and force them to comply.

7. Operate the largest Slaek Device he had ever seen in a hidden facility to drop guns in different Budaiynorean revolutionary rebel camps. An act that was likely to start a war in the Eastern hemisphere. Elbaz did not tell him the

exact purpose of this mission or how it even related to Slaek-Cities, despite having told him that this mission's success was of the highest importance.

Desmond groaned to himself as he entered The Hotel. With so much to do in such a short span of time, he could not afford to enjoy the rare breaks from work he was getting. He could not sit still without his mind flashing forward to the vast intricacies and subtle minutiae that had to be ironed out beforehand to make sure each of those missions either achieved their intended goal or, at the very least, failed in a way that they could be re-tried and completed at a later date.

Desmond now knew what it meant for there to be 'no rest for the wicked.' Since he had risen to the rank of Elbaz's heir, he had not been able to rest his body for a second. A minor slip meant a major fallout in both of their careers.

The young Elbaz successor possessed no energy to even walk to his room. His feet almost buckled beneath him as he resigned himself to the white seating in The Hotel's lobby just a few steps away from the entrance.

As soon as his body touched the plush, pristine seating, he sank into it. Falling asleep in the lobby of the living quarters of most RealSlaek employees was asking for trouble. But Desmond did not care. Nor could he control himself even if he had cared. His eyelids grew heavy, closing as he took a deep breath and accepted the oncoming slumber.

"Desmond! Is that you sleeping there?!" another young man called out to him, laughing.

He opened his eyes, throwing any chances of getting some rest as he forced himself to engage with whoever approached him. He saw a face he had not seen around RealSlaek in a while, especially due to his various rapid promotions in position. Jack Kashworth, one of the first friends he made at the company. The man he met at the integration event, where he had first seen Chantelle. A living reminder of relatively simpler times when he was a fresh employee. Back when he could actually hope to have a moment of peace to himself from time to time.

"Jack. How are you doing, man?"

"I'm doing really good. How are you?"

"Doing well."

Jack laughed. "You don't look it. You're drained!"

Desmond sighed. "Yeah, I am drained, to be honest."

"Must be the extra work. I'm a little jealous."

"You're jealous of the extra work that's draining me?"

"Fuck yeah! You're the big man around here!" Jack laughed. "Some older employees were talking about you, and they said they've only seen one other person who rose through the ranks as fast! You're something else!"

"I appreciate that," Desmond chuckled weakly. "But sometimes I wish I'd risen more gradually, you know? Then maybe I'd have the energy to actually walk back to my room instead of sleeping in the damn lobby."

Jack chuckled. "I remember when you were brand new to this company. When all of us in our section were. It feels like we were drinking cognac together at that integration event just yesterday!"

"Yeah, I was just thinking about that. That was the same night I got with Chantelle, even though you advised against it," Desmond said.

"That's funny. Don't know what I was so worried about back then," Jack recalled, shaking his head with a smile. "Look at you and Chantelle now! From what I've heard, you've got a great thing going together!"

"True, things are going well for us," Desmond said.

194

For some reason, none of the bright, wonderful, and emotional parts of his and Chantelle's relationship passed through his mind. All he could think about was how they helped each other murder Margot and Lloyd without facing any justice for their crimes. It excited him more than anything else they had been through together.

"I need to go now, man. I've got an important mission coming up," Jack said.

"What mission?" Desmond asked.

"A couple of us have been tasked with screening the guy who will be replacing MacGowan's role in the company," Jack stated.

"Sean MacGowan's gone?" Desmond asked, surprised but hopeful. Ever since Desmond's rapid series of promotions, the RealSlaek head had been much kinder to him. But he still held a grudge over how he acted during his early days. Especially at the blackmail-reveal dinner when he mocked him for having caused his siblings' deaths. It was cathartic to hear he would no longer be around. He liked to think that if he had truly left the company, he would probably be killed soon. "Why? What happened with him?"

"The ginger bastard died," Jack laughed.

Desmond gasped with fake sorrow. The news delighted him. "Shit, really? How?"

"His chest was crushed in an incredibly weird and unlucky accident a few days ago. Apparently, a car with no driver spun out of control and slammed into him outside a sushi restaurant. People are saying Slaek Devices were involved. Seemed kind of fishy, but I didn't care enough to look into it myself," Jack explained. "Anyway, I need to go, I'm going to be late for the pre-mission prep. See ya."

"See you later," Desmond said as Jack left.

Desmond remained glued to his position for the next hour. He only bothered to rise from his seat once he saw Chantelle pass the reception desk.

His girlfriend was dressed to the nines and looked to be heading in the direction of his room. She changed course once she saw him in the lobby.

"Why aren't you in your room getting ready?" she asked as she approached him.

"What am I meant to be getting ready for?" he asked. Chantelle groaned. "You forgot?" she pouted. "We're supposed to have dinner at Nus Et Kanasrericka tonight!"

Desmond sighed. "I did forget," he admitted. "I've had so much work to do and future missions to think about. It passed through my mind completely. Sorry, love."

"It's alright," Chantelle sighed with a smile. She stood on her tip-toes to give Desmond a pecked kiss on his forehead. "It's hard being the star of the company, isn't it, dear?"

"You know it," Desmond said, forcing a smile on his fatigued face.

TEST, MOTHER

THE TEST. President Elbaz emailed Desmond out of the blue that morning, asking him to come to the grey-site office. He reminded him of last month's meeting, where Desmond asked him about the phases of his vision that followed the mass installations of Slaek-Cities across the globe. He told Desmond he would need to test him first before he felt ready to divulge. The day of the test had arrived.

Desmond stepped into the president's wardrobe-cluttered office, almost as nervous as he had been on his first-ever visit. He pulled out the chair across from the president, who lay back in his chair, looking to the ceiling where a Slaek Device floated a gold coin. As Desmond took his seat, the coin dropped. Elbaz caught it and folded his arms in the same movement as he attended to Desmond.

"It's test time," Elbaz chuckled to him.

"So it is," Desmond responded, quiet and stern.

Elbaz stood behind the table. "What do you reckon I've got in store for you, Eze?"

"No clue."

"Guess."

"Well, some kind of test of character? Something that will prove my will and conviction?"

"Yes, exactly that, especially the part about will and conviction. Do you have any guesses that are more specific?"

"Not at all."

Elbaz walked to one of the wardrobes that lined his walls.

"Don't worry. It's nothing flashy or complex. It's a very simple, straightforward test. The first that came to mind, but the best out of the list I spent all night drafting," he chuckled. "Why am I still talking? It's best I just show you already!"

With a fastened-shut mouth, rising goosebumps, and a sigh out of his nose, Desmond prepared himself mentally for the test. He watched as Ezra used a Slaek Device to open the locks of one of the imposing wardrobes surrounding them. No amount of mental preparation would have readied Desmond's mind for what he saw next.

The body of an unconscious woman dropped out of the wardrobe. The president caught this person with a smile. Desmond threw himself out of his chair, rising with outrage.

"What the fuck?!" he exclaimed. "That-, that's-"

"Your mother? Yes," Elbaz answered, propping up the drugged and sleeping Mrs Eze. "I recently found out about how you reconnected with her a few months ago, around the same time your grandmother passed away. I know that you've talked to her here and there since then, but haven't made proper plans to fully involve yourselves in each other's lives yet. I wouldn't bother with that moving forward."

"What have you done with her?! What are you *planning* on doing to her?!" Desmond asked, shouting out.

Ezra chortled. "I haven't done and don't plan on doing anything with Mrs Eze, aside from drugging her and bringing her here. You're the one who will be *doing things* to her.

That's the test," Elbaz stated with a deranged grin as he threw her on the table. "Mutilate your mother, Desmond Eze. In whatever way you see fit. Defile her body and kill her. I'll decide if you pass based on how well you do both."

Desmond watched as the body of the woman who birthed him slumped over the table. Dregs of drool spilt out of the corners of her mouth, her chest moving slightly through snoring breaths.

"You're joking. You have to be," Desmond said, chuckling nervously. Elbaz gave him that look again. That rare look of complete seriousness. Utter solemnity.

"Wait, I figured out the real test! You want to see if I'll just blindly follow your orders, don't you, sir? Because I won't!" Desmond said.

"No, that is not the real test, Desmond," Elbaz scoffed. "Ruin your mother's body, then end her life. Or do the second first and the first second. Just hurry up. Make sure you do it all. Right here, right now."

Desmond glared at Elbaz, bewildered beyond disbelief. He could not comprehend the scenario he had been placed in. He kept telling himself that the president was clearly joking, that this was an obvious, eccentrically sadistic jape that he was taking too far. But then he would look back into the president's dark eyes. The comforting pupils that quelled the woes of a nation were darker than any killer eyes he had ever seen at RealSlaek. He meant every single word he had uttered. The test was real. He was expected to defile and murder his own mother.

"What's the problem? I thought you wanted to be my successor? I thought you agreed you could rise to the occasion?" Ezra shouted, laughing. "This is a part of being

Elbaz, you know. My mum died because of me! Yours is going to die because of you!"

"You killed your mother by accident as a child! Diseases contracted due to childbirth are *not* the same as whatever shit you're trying to make me do here!" Desmond shouted back.

Ezra scowled as if he had only now remembered this crucial fact of his life. "Yes, I suppose you're right. But I *did* intentionally murder my father! It was the first thing I did when I started my political career at nineteen. The second I developed deep enough connections to get away with it, I had the man 'back-doored' as gangsters say!" Elbaz explained with glee. "So, if you're going to be like me, you need to kill your mother! Then, we'll both have a dead mother *and* be responsible for the murder of a parent! It'll match!"

"Jesus Christ, what the fuck is wrong with you?!" Desmond exclaimed. "You're fucking absurd! I'm not going through with any of this! Successor or not!"

"I don't want to start throwing around threats or anything, but I hope you realise what will happen if you don't do as I say," the president warned.

Desmond's heart pounded with force as Elbaz's evil eyes lasered in on him. A contorting pain in his chest made it hard for him to stand straight and breathe.

"No. No. I won't do it," Desmond said weakly.

"No?! What's '*no*'?! You don't have a fucking choice! This is the test!" Elbaz yelled.

"No…"

"Yes! Destroy this woman's withered ageing body, then slit her throat! Do it or I'll have worse done to you!"

"Sir, please…"

"Sir, please," Elbaz repeated, mocking Desmond's voice in a whiny pitch. "No pleading! Only defiling, cutting, and killing! Do it to her or I'll do it to you! With just one call, I'll get my guards in here, and they'll do things to your body you won't even believe are possible! If you don't fuck up your mother right goddamn now, you're going to end up as a bloody pile of flesh on the news!"

Desmond shook his head. He could feel himself getting dizzy, lightening. He felt his body weaken, knowing it would not be long until he started hyperventilating. He desperately tried to keep a clear head. He tried to figure out a way out of this situation. But nothing came to mind.

"Here! If you don't know where to start, I'll help you!" Elbaz shouted. A Slaek Device floated a knife out of the open wardrobe and into his hand.

Desmond dove over his mother and the table, tackling the president to the ground. His body acted before his mind could even think as he threw himself and his country's leader into a crashing thud against the back wardrobe.

"How dare you?! You attack me?! Me?! Are you feeling extra brave today, is that it?!" Elbaz screamed. He struggled against Desmond, scratching and clawing at him to force his release. Desmond forced him to back down into submission with a cracking headbutt. "Ah, my fucking nose! You dare bloody my bloody fucking nose?!" Elbaz cried.

"I'll bloody it again!" Desmond threatened.

"Attacking a man of my position will get you sentenced to death, you know that?!" Elbaz yelped.

"I don't give a shit!" Desmond exclaimed, headbutting him again. "You were going to hurt my mother, so I don't fucking care what happens! I'm going to hurt you!"

Elbaz laughed nasally through the pain of his battered nose and mouth. "It's over for you! You attacked me! You made me fucking bleed! You're not leaving this room alive!

You're fucking done!" he shouted in a frantic, frothing tirade, screaming in between laughs.

"I don't know why you're fucking laughing! You're not leaving this room alive either!" Desmond shouted back.

He saw Elbaz's arm raise with the Slaek Device on his hand activating. Before the president could summon anything, Desmond grabbed his wrist and twisted it with the most strength he had ever applied to anything in his life. The president screamed, his hand dropping, broken and limp. Desmond shut him up with a punch to the mouth. The president groaned in pain, his eyes a dizzying glaze as he thrashed about the floor. Desmond sought to end him, wrapping both hands around his neck and squeezing tightly.

"FUCK YOU AND FUCK SLAEK!" Desmond screamed as he wrung Elbaz's neck.

The door to the office burst open. In poured a dozen bodyguards, finally responding to the commotion in the room. President Elbaz was saved from being choked to death as multiple guards tore Desmond from him.

The adrenaline left Desmond's body as he was taken off the president and robbed of his dozenth political murder. It would have been his greatest since joining RealSlaek.

Desmond accepted his fate, allowing the bodyguards to restrain him against the wardrobe. In spite of what he knew was about to happen to him, he had no regrets. It was all he could think of doing in that moment. No matter what feelings he once had about his mother, killing her was the last thing he would ever do. If that was what he had to do in order to secure his position in Elbaz's eyes, then that was a position that was not worth even the most worldly of accolades.

It made him physically sick to think that was once his goal. To become like him. He once considered him to be the brightest world leader of them all. But now he saw President Ezra Elbaz as the darkest, most disgusting devil spawn to ever crawl out of a woman and into the world.

He cursed himself internally for only accepting this fact now. It should have been clear to him from the start. From the moment he realised he was RealSlaek RF's greatest investor, he should have known the depths of depravity such a man would sink to, and that he would try to drag him down with him. He was glad he had finally come to his senses. If he had to die because of this, then so be it.

The rest of the bodyguards helped Elbaz back on his feet. He rubbed his bruised neck with his unbroken hand. One of the bodyguards gave him a bottle of water to drink as the others tended to his limp wrist. Desmond watched in fearful anticipation as Elbaz drank the water, the president staring at him the entire time. Once he finished, Elbaz put the empty bottle on the desk next to Mrs Eze.

The president walked around the table towards Desmond and the guards. He stood a few inches from him. His everyday smile returned to his face.

"Congratulations," Elbaz chuckled. "You passed."
Desmond's face dropped. "What?!" he exclaimed.

"You passed the test! And with flying colours! This is much better than anything I expected from you!" Elbaz celebrated with his hands in the air. "I wish I could replay that scene like it was a movie! There you were, ready to kill the most powerful man in the world, all because you didn't want to hurt your mother! If that's not conviction, then I don't know what is! Marvellous! Absolutely fucking marvellous!"

Desmond's mind was in even more of a mess than it had been throughout that entire stressful ordeal. He could not differentiate north from south if asked to in that moment. He had no hope of wrapping his head around all that was happening in front of him. "What?!" he repeated.

Elbaz grabbed Desmond by the back of his neck and gave him a kiss on his lips. He rambled on.

"Forget Slaek-Cities, you're going to help me build Slaek-Countries! We'll usher in all sorts together! Fully autonomous Slaek-Robots! Self-piloting Slaek-installed planes and large-scale spacecraft! Miniature Slaek Devices that can be implanted underneath skin and controlled from our bases! There's so much to plan! We'll use this company to change the world forever!" Elbaz boomed, as animated as a human being could be. "Phase after phase, world project after world project, you're going to be by my side! You're going to watch as my vision comes to fruition. And then, when the time comes, you'll enact visions of your own!"

Desmond squinted, his mouth gaping in a gormless sigh as he watched Elbaz prance around. The president spun, jumped, and twirled as if he were a mischievous creature from a cautionary fairytale.

"I couldn't have asked for a better successor!" Elbaz cheered. "God bless you, Desmond Eze!"

***

Desmond sat on his bed next to his resting mother. She was awake and slowly recovering from being drugged unconscious by Elbaz.

This was the first time his mother had seen or entered his RealSlaek apartment. Desmond wished it did not have to be on this day. He wore the face of an eternally confused man, having still not recovered from Elbaz's test hours ago. All he could focus on was taking care of his mother.

"I don't know what happened, I must have overworked myself," his mum said to him. "It's scary passing out like that. I'm glad you came to pick me up, sweetheart."

"Yeah," Desmond said mindlessly.

"I had a weird fever dream whilst I was out. A very peculiar man approached me and told me he was your boss," Mrs Eze said. "He looked similar to President Elbaz. Isn't that strange?"

"Yeah," Desmond answered mindlessly.

Mrs Eze glanced at the walls of his room, astonished by the white coating of the area. Something as mundane as that was enough to impress her. They were leagues beyond the type of walls most of the Eze family had been used to living within.

"This is very nice. I'm surprised RealSlaek allows their employees to live in homes this lovely without having to pay any rent," she commented. "You're really lucky."

"Yeah," Desmond agreed mindlessly. "I am."

RETROSPECT, REMEMBER

THE 2020s. A period that historians of Alterna-Earth looked back on with intrigue and sorrow. The first half was infamous for being the beginning of the CM Era. An era in which President Ezra Elbaz of Renyland used multiple different applications of the powerful substance of Slaek to make countless pieces of technology that changed humanity even after his reign. Another man often cited as a proponent of the demise brought on by the CM era was Desmond Eze, the powerful CEO of RealSlaek RF.

Tales of history told that during the early 2020s, Desmond was nothing more than a RealSlaek RF employee with slight connections to President Elbaz. But by the end of the decade, he controlled the company and was considered one of Elbaz's closest allies, closer than any other figure.

These were the men to blame for the worsening of the world. If you had told men of previous eras that they would wake up every day in cramped Slaek-City vessels, they would not believe you. If you told them they would have their every move observed and manipulated by devices forcibly applied under their very skin, they would not believe you. If you told them they would struggle to feed their families or find any form of life purpose due to almost every occupation or important task being overtaken by the advanced self-directed technology of a single company, they would not have believed you. Yet this was the reality of every human being during the CM Era and decades after that, thanks to Elbaz and Eze's efforts. The atomised, despondent, constantly-surveyed, passionless, weak, desperate, Slaek-controlled state of humanity for decades upon decades was the fault of these two men and their machinations.

President Ezra Elbaz did not live a long life. He was killed in a tragic car accident in the year 2036. Desmond Eze, however, did. He was noted to have thrived well into old age, having fathered and raised five children during that time with his wife Chantelle Belle, another high-ranking RSRF employee who rose to greater power after the 2020s.

Desmond Eze suffered no consequences for the damage he had done to the world. The crimes he and Elbaz committed would not come to light until a decade after his death.

When the truth came out, his name was marked in history along with Elbaz's. Humans of Alterna-Earth knew them as the men whose misuse of Slaek almost destroyed their world. A fact that would never be forgotten.

THE AUTHOR

Jason Boje is a Nigerian-European author of thriller, drama, fantasy, crime, and science fiction novels. He graduated with a Bachelor of Arts with Honours degree in Business Economics from Lancaster University in 2023, where he had developed his writing skills alongside his studies over the years. He has received numerous awards for several written works, including television screenplays and online novels.

CONNECT WITH JASON VIA:

Instagram: @jasonbojewriting

TikTok: @jasonbojewriting

YouTube: @jasonbtg